PRAISE FOR GRAHAM LIRONI

"An intelligent, original and disturbing new voice in Scottish fiction." A L KENNEDY

"A haunting and original piece of work, a cult book in the making." THE HERALD

"The new bad boy of Scottish fiction is misbehaving very well indeed.... has the pace, intensity and cultural referencing of a literary Pulp Fiction." THE LIST

"A slick unfussy writer who keeps things moving to their sticky end." SUNDAY HERALD

"Graham Lironi is for real." THE SCOTSMAN

Oh Marina Girl

the death sentence of a spaceman

Graham Lironi

CONTRABAND

Contraband is an imprint of Saraband

Published by Saraband
Suite 202, 98 Woodlands Road
Glasgow, G3 6HB
www.saraband.net

ISBN: 9781908643919
ebook: 9781908643926

Printed in the EU on sustainably sourced paper.

1 2 3 4 5 6 19 18 17 16 15

For my family,
At long last, it spirals out now.

'In the beginning was the word. Its letters were a string of amino acids that spelt the genesis of life. The letters multiplied enormously and now come in whole libraries that we pass on to our descendants.'

PAUL PETER PIECH

Contents

PART ONE

i am not he

chapter one

the spaceman

THAT FATEFUL MORNING BEGAN like any other weekday of the past decade: I rolled out of bed, gulped down cornflakes, show-ered, shaved, shit, caught the number 44 bus into work, scanned the paper en route, squeezed into the crowded lift (despite my claustrophobia) to the first floor and, unable to resist the temp-tation, before I even removed my coat and hat, stopped and glanced at the translucent purple paperweight pinning down the pile of letters on my desk.

The letters hadn't always drowned me in apathy; there was a time when they'd stirred me with enthusiasm — but that was long ago when I was a fresh-faced raw recruit fired with ambi-tion. Possessed with a shiny new evangelical zeal, I'd fancied I was embarking on a moral crusade that would expose the city's corrupt underbelly. My zeal had long since been buried beneath a thickening layer of apathy and I'd become resigned to watching the spread of the corruption all around me.

Apathy was invariably the cause of any occasional mistake made by myself; but I was fortunate in that I'd made only one serious error in my career to date when I'd unintentionally hit the space bar when writing about a therapist so that instead of the sentence reading, 'Therapist John McDonald...', it read, 'The rapist John McDonald...'.

The newspaper, a broadsheet, had national ambitions, but its circulation was confined largely to the city where it was produced. Its local news coverage outweighed its national news coverage which outweighed its international news coverage. The letters, I knew before opening them, would reflect this weighting of local, national and international concerns.

The exception to this rule of parochialism occurred periodically with the onset of exceptional circumstances, such as those prevailing at present, with Britain having just committed itself to participation in the resolution of a bloody conflict between opposing ethnic groups in central Europe; a commitment made on the basis of the laudable humanitarian principle that it is unacceptable for us as a nation to sit idly by whilst an undemocratic regime headed by a bloodthirsty tyrant repeatedly ignores all United Nations appeals to reason and proceeds to invade its bordering nation's territory to carry out a systematic slaughter of its neighbours in an attempt to render extinct an entire race.

Newspapers relish such exceptional circumstances: publishers rejoice in the sudden surge in circulation figures; journalists revel in the opportunity to express their moral indignation and the sense of self-worth that reporting such events gives them. I am exceptional in my distinct lack of enthusiasm.

You see, the day before's front page, and several inside pages, had been devoted to an examination of the ramifications of the announcement of Britain's involvement in the escalating international crisis and I knew that, for the foreseeable future, whilst the quantity of letters landing on my desk would multiply, their diversity would contract into two opposing camps: those from readers writing to express their support for Britain's intervention and those opposed to it, so that, whilst journalists discovered their *raison d'être*, I discovered new peaks of monotony.

Of course, none of the letters were addressed to me personally. Rather, they were addressed to 'the letters page' and dumped on my desk for me to open.

This was a process I wouldn't begin until I'd removed my raincoat and jacket, taken off my homburg, hung up my umbrella and ventured into the kitchen to make myself a cup of peppermint tea.

That morning, I found myself occupying the space between the parallel universes of a pair of overripe bottle-blonde cultural commentators — engrossed in a voluble conversation on remedies for period pain — and a pair of teenage sports correspondents, engrossed in an equally voluble conversation about the implications of the result of the previous evening's match on the eventual outcome of the league, and how it had turned on a woeful performance by the referee who had blown his whistle for an offside that clearly wasn't but failed to blow it for a penalty that clearly was. Obviously their favoured team had lost.

Both the cultural commentators and the 'sports' (which in Glasgow was a term synonymous with 'football') correspondents appeared oblivious to events outwith their own particular areas of expertise; such as the fact that we were on the brink of entering into a war.

'Morning.'

Both parallel conversations stopped abruptly and I looked up from stirring my tea to see the occupants of the kitchen waiting for me to respond.

'Morning,' I obliged.

'How's the missus?' asked Kirsty Baird, the more buxom of the blondes.

'Fine,' I lied, 'she's fine.'

This had been my standard response since the first morning I returned to work a few days after receiving Lisa's first and last letter. It was an automatic defence mechanism designed to deflect from divulging the truth; a ruse deployed out of recognition that the truth was not always the desired response in matters of everyday social etiquette.

Lisa had never been my missus. She'd insisted on a Catholic wedding ceremony and I'd insisted on a registrar office until the subject was consigned to the burgeoning list of taboos spread out between us, all interlinked by faith and faithlessness, separating us by its immovable bulk.

No, Lisa had never been my missus. She was one of my two *misses* — the other was Andy — and the space left by their absence defined me.

I decided it was time I started slitting some envelopes, an everyday function which, over years of monotonous repetition, had become endowed with the solemnity of a sacramental rite. I performed this ritual with a letter opener that masqueraded as a traditional Highland knife, or skean dhu. Lisa had given it to me long ago when I'd first landed this job.

Nobody could slit an envelope like me. I'd perfected it into an art form, gutting it with one swift slash.

But before I'd start slitting, I'd put on my tortoiseshell specs, after wiping the lenses with a hankie to which I'd applied a sliver of saliva, boot up the computer to start printing out the e-mails (I refuse to ruin what's left of my failing eyesight by squinting at a reflective screen), shuffle and staple the faxes and rifle through the envelopes in the hope of discovering an exotic postmark. By this time my tea will have cooled sufficiently to allow me my first slurp.

I never start to read the letters until I've disembowelled all the envelopes. When this is done, I'll open the letters out, place them in a neat pile and contemplate them, sipping my tea. There was a time when my taste buds had savoured the peppermint prospect of what priceless pearls of wisdom the pile before me might contain, but that was long ago and the piles had long since lost their flavour.

Only once I'd drained my cup did I buckle down to the task of reading.

It was a task within which I'd immerse myself until noon, at which time I'd pick up my umbrella, don my raincoat and homburg, take the lift down to the ground floor and stroll to the

Mitchell Library to while away an hour browsing amongst books on calligraphy.

Given the monotony of my job, it was perhaps inevitable that I should become a self-taught, and sometimes subconscious, graphologist. Scrutinising the endless flow of scribbles lassoed by extravagant loops, and the indecipherable signatures, to construct my personality profile of various letter writers.

But I'd recently become intrigued by the spaces between the words as much as the words themselves. You see, I began to notice some time ago, and I've been fascinated by it since, that, however different our handwriting might be, the gap we leave between our words is always consistent. We do this automatically — or at least we did — because, now that I've pointed it out to you, you probably can't help but be conscious of the gap *you* leave.

It's not unusual for me to finish a letter only to realise that I've immediately forgotten what I've just read. The clearest example of this I can recall was when I was so disturbed by the calligraphy of a particular letter that I became convinced that its author was a potential murderer, only to discover, after having read it for the third time, that the letter was, in fact, a confession to matricide.

But, from the very start, the content of one of this morning's letters grabbed my full attention — perhaps because of its anonymity (literally — there was no signature; and calligraphically — it was written on bog-standard foolscap with a bog-standard blue biro). Yet there was also something familiar about the handwriting which I couldn't quite pinpoint.

When I finished it I glanced over at my colleagues to check that they were engrossed in their own screens or conversations, then refolded it and slipped it into the breast pocket of my stiff-collared, white Bri-Nylon shirt.

I attempted to resume my letter reading, but no matter how extravagant the loops and hoops, how intriguing the signature, it was the letter burning through my shirt pocket that I was rereading.

Apart from the handwriting, one other particular aspect of the letter perplexed me all morning — though I realised it would only be me for whom it was a puzzle. Then, when the umpteenth trawl through my bin failed to find a disembowelled and discarded matching envelope stamped with an identifiable postmark I belatedly perceived to be of paramount importance, a possible explanation to the puzzle finally dawned on me.

I gasped, cursed myself under my breath, ran to the library an hour earlier than usual, forgetting my umbrella in my haste to confirm the solution to the puzzle, causing some consternation amongst those of my colleagues who set their watches by the precision of the hitherto meticulous routine I had just abandoned with such uncharacteristic impetuousness.

I suppose it would be easier for you to understand my actions if I explained the content of the letter to you. In fact, I can do better than that — I can reproduce it for you verbatim:

Intolerance will not be tolerated.

Following the publication of his letter in yesterday's paper, I have taken hostage Ian Thome. I will slit his throat unless you publish this letter, unedited, on the front page of tomorrow morning's paper and promise never again to publish such a misguided defence of pernicious propaganda. Failure to do so will result in your own capture and execution.

Do not contact the police. Do take this threat seriously. Remember what happened to Craig Liddell.

Whilst this verbatim reproduction of the letter will no doubt give you some inkling of why it received my full and horrified attention, since you are presently unaware of the context within which it was written and the people referred to in it, it will probably make little sense to you. Nor will it be clear to you what, specifically, puzzled me.

chapter two

verbatim

FIRSTLY, let me tell you a little about Craig Liddell.

Although I had no more than a passing acquaintance with Liddell, several of my colleagues had known him well — the city centre is sufficiently condensed to enable the more sociable members of the fraternity of those who earn their daily bread from the written word to congregate in cliques outwith office hours.

I was on the periphery of this incestuous circle — partly through choice (over recent years it had become infested with a plague of PR parasites who had infiltrated it with the objective of buying drinks for the circle's other members with their paymaster's moolah and bending the ears of the circle's other members with their paymaster's propaganda in the hope that it would subsequently appear in print the following day. More often than not it did, but I preferred to restrict my relations with such practitioners of the dark arts to a strictly professional basis, uncomfortable with the notion that the cultivation of friendships could only compromise my precious editorial integrity), partly through my lowly status as a letters page editor (it was not a position overburdened with kudos — which suited me fine since it meant that I didn't have succeeding generations of overeager graduates fighting amongst themselves to replace me, unwittingly driving down the potential remuneration package through their competitive zeal), but mostly because of my unsociable preference for spending my lunch hour browsing amongst books of calligraphy in the Mitchell Library rather than contributing to the gossip masquerading as wheeling and dealing that takes place over extended lunch time G&Ts at the Space Bar (a name that ensured that I would never be permitted to forget my unfortunate faux pas).

Liddell had been a book reviewer on a lifestyle magazine, which made him an integral member of the incestuous circle. He had the kudos I lacked, the sociability I lacked and the ability to cultivate friendships with the PR parasites without allowing them to compromise his integrity, which I lacked.

If that sounds like I envied him then that's because I did — but I certainly don't envy what happened to him.

Liddell had a reputation amongst his fellow critics for being acerbic but fair, which meant that he had a reputation amongst authors for being scathing and unfair (though this grudge was seldom, if ever, shared by the author's own PR parasites who, having already written off any given book, and with one eye already on the next launch for the next author on a burgeoning list, without exception confided to Liddell that, strictly off the record, they concurred with his criticisms).

It was only a month since Liddell had been killed and the reactions to his murder had dominated the letters page for days afterwards. My paper, and its competitors, had reported and analysed the incident in depth. This had, after all, been regarded by those members of the incestuous circle as an attack on one of its own; an attack on the very principle that allowed them to tell themselves that they were employed in a noble profession; an attack on what gave a purpose to their lives.

In the month since he was slain, Liddell had already become a martyr to the ideal of free speech.

The high regard with which he'd been held by his peer group was confirmed by the swift establishment of a memorial fund that was soon swollen with generous donations seeking to provide financial security for the wife and daughter who survived him (he'd been the household's sole breadwinner, his wife having adopted the role of full-time nurse to their mentally handicapped daughter, and he had died intestate with only modest savings to his name).

Liddell had been found slumped in the armchair of a room in the Holiday Inn, his hands bound behind his back, his throat sliced and with a small hatchet lodged in his forehead. Judging by the amount of blood, which had clogged his body to the armchair, oozed down his trouser legs and trickled over his brogues to congeal on a fake fur white rug, some hours had passed before his body had been discovered by a maid's routine visit to clean the room.

The hotel register revealed that the room — a single with an uninterrupted view of a brick wall — had been booked in the name of Toni Mahe, who had paid by cash and checked out shortly before the discovery of Liddell's corpse.

Mahe's name was suspected by the detectives investigating the murder to be false. This suspicion was reinforced by the discovery that the address Mahe had scrawled in the hotel register was fictitious.

Liddell's murderer had yet to be identified and the motive for the murder yet to be established, though umpteen conspiracy theories had flourished in the month since it had occurred. These ranged from the fanciful (a revenge attack perpetrated by an unhinged and overly-sensitive-to-the-point-of-paranoid author bearing a grudge against a savage review of his masterpiece) to the sordid (a secret sado-masochistic sex romp with an unknown prostitute — male or female, take your pick — with homicidal tendencies) but all, in some way or another, failed to provide a satisfactory explanation for Liddell's murder.

So much for Craig Liddell. What about the alleged 'misguided defence of pernicious propaganda' of Ian Thome's letter, which had evidently prompted his kidnapper to abduct him?

Once again, it might help you reach your own conclusions about Thome's letter if I reproduce it for you verbatim. That way you can decide for yourself if it is indeed a 'defence of intolerance' or, rather, a reasoned argument simply put.

Dear Sir,

I feel that Ms Toe's review of Original Harm, *the debut novel from Tom Haine, was based on a misreading of the text.*

Whilst the book addresses the subject of abortion, which is a matter of life or death, the author neither seeks to steer his readers down a path leading to one particular point of view nor shirks from presenting his own.

Contrary to Ms Toe, I happen to share the standpoint of Igor Harmnail, the narrative's improbably-named anti-hero, that 'life is no more nor less than a sexually transmitted terminal condition' and that, 'from the womb to the tomb, from abortion to euthanasia, whenever they find themselves confronted with a moral dilemma and faced with making a decision between right and wrong, the faithful are nothing if not consistent in their uncanny ability to always get it wrong'.

I may speak from the luxury of never having to face the dilemma myself and, arguably, that very fact disqualifies my opinion from serious consideration but, just maybe, my impartiality permits the application of reason without the potent, yet poisonous, potion of doctrine and emotion to cloud the issue.

The fact that Ms Toe is of a different sex to myself seems sufficient, in her opinion, for her to dismiss my views as irrelevant. Whilst she is, of course, entitled to her views, a book review seems an inappropriate place to express them and it is quite unprofessional for her to mount her soapbox at Haine's expense. My suspicion is that Toe had her own personal agenda at play here and was guilty of grinding her axe at the expense of the dispassionate professionalism such an emotive subject deserves and requires.

But, contrary to Toe's superficial reading, Original Harm is not simply a book about abortion; rather, it concerns itself with the hijacking of such dilemmas by moral terrorists who swallow the dangerously nonsensical credo that ends justify means.

Finally, Toe is apparently ignorant of the factual context which served as Haines's inspiration for the book. For, whilst the dramatisation, and much of the characterisation, is fictional, Original Harm is based on a true story.

Yours,
Ian Thome

So much for the letter. Hardly sufficient to prompt a kidnapping, don't you think? Thome's letter contains, certainly, a defence, but whether or not it constitutes a defence of 'pernicious propaganda' you are not as yet at liberty to judge.

So, what? I'm conscious of the fact that, rather than enlightening you, the reproduction of this letter has probably, at this stage, succeeded only in baffling you further. If you can bear with me for a little longer, I'll endeavour to explain the context, as I see it, which led to these extraordinary events.

You will have gathered that Ms Toe is the name of the author of the review of *Original Harm* that had inspired Thome's letter to the editor. Toe, whose first name is Niamh, is an occasional freelance book reviewer for the paper.

Of course, you remain unable to state categorically whether this letter is a 'misguided defence of pernicious propaganda' or a reasoned argument because you are unfamiliar with *Original Harm* and its review.

Let's take the review first. Once again, I'll reproduce it for you verbatim (it really is the only way to avoid misinterpretation):

It is often said that the first and most important lesson writers learn is to write about what they know. Tom Haine has chosen abortion as the subject for his debut novel; a subject of which he seems singularly ill-equipped to write about meaningfully. He reveals next to no medical knowledge about the subject throughout his text; offers no comment on the stance (contemporary or historical) adopted towards abortion by the Church or Westminster or Holyrood; appears ignorant of the current relevant legislation; clearly has had no direct or indirect personal experience of abortion and, as a consequence of all these factors, brings no fresh insights to bear on the debate.

Frankly, I, for one, found his muddled little lily-livered arguments offensive and unhelpful.

All this could, arguably, be forgiven if only Original Harm could be shown to shine under the light of an analysis restricted strictly to literary merits but, alas, even under that artificially confined examination, it proves dull reading: its prose is turgid; its plot twists tortured; its characters one-dimensional stereotypes.

If Haine has a talent, it is for threatening to deaden the acutely felt physical and mental pain of the reality of abortion under the anaesthetic of his banal prose.

Perhaps if he had been a she and could write with his heart as well as his head, this book would have some merit. Unfortunately, Original Harm has no merit whatsoever.

As it is obviously impractical to reproduce Haine's novel verbatim, for reasons of copyright as much as reasons of space, I won't. Instead, I'll reproduce the summary that appears on its flyleaf (which is, of course, written with the express purpose of arousing your curiosity and enticing you to read the text — i.e. it could not be more biased).

A gang of self-styled purists known as The Amino beats a doctor to death outside his clinic. The victim, who had been on his way to the hospital to help in the delivery of his second child, had written a defence of the existing legalisation of abortion in the previous day's newspaper. The doctor's wife gives birth to a boy less than an hour after her husband's savage beating.

Not only is Original Harm *a carefully constructed thriller/ killer; it's a crafted commentary on the absurdity lurking at the core of conventionality; a sly slant on the surreality of reality and an all-too pertinent parable for the present, pondering the tolerance of intolerance and the intolerance of tolerance.*

You will perhaps have already guessed that it is the beating referred to in the flyleaf, which is based on the 'true story', referred to in Thome's letter.

It is a matter of historical record that at precisely 11:33am on the morning of February 11 1992 in this very city, a Dr Joseph Kirk was attacked and beaten to death outside his clinic on his way to help in the delivery of his second child.

So just who is this Tom Haine character anyway? Well, no photo or autobiographical information about him is given on the jacket of *Original Harm*. The author appears to revel in anonymity.

chapter three

a tight spot

SO MUCH FOR CONTEXT. Whether I've clarified or muddled things further for you I don't know. Let's return to the fateful events of the other morning.

You'll recall that I departed from my routine to rush to the Mitchell in a state of some consternation. At the library I scurried to the general reference section and yanked two thick phone books from a packed shelf, one listing the numbers of residents with surnames ranging from the letters L to Z located south of the Clyde, the second, of residents with corresponding surnames located north. My freshly licked fingers, trembling with trepidation, turned the pages of the first volume then traced down a row of names.

When they failed to find the particular name they were searching for, this volume was discarded and they grabbed the second volume. However, again unable to locate the name they were seeking, my by-now inky fingertips were soon expressing their perplexity by drumming on the desktop, a habit which halted when I realised that the page where the particular surname I sought (and dreaded finding) would have been listed was missing.

I returned to the office as quickly as I could to consult a copy of the same volume (why hadn't I saved myself the trip to the library and consulted the office volume earlier? Two reasons. Firstly, I didn't know which phone directory would list the name I was seeking and the selection of directories at the library was far more extensive than those at the office. Secondly, I sought to conceal my consternation from my colleagues) and confirm my worst fears.

On my way back to the office I had an uneasy feeling that I was being watched, a feeling which, though I was unable to verify it, lingered until it solidified into a conviction. It occurred to me that I'd managed to entangle myself in something of a tight spot.

Back at my desk, my worst fears were confirmed when I located the name I'd been seeking. This solved the puzzle of the letter and put me in a very tight spot indeed. Cursing my recklessness, I reread the letter for the umpteenth time that morning — the familiarity of the calligraphy continued to niggle me — then scribbled down the number and address from the phone book and glanced at my watch. There was hardly any time to think. What could I do? I tried the number. It rang out. I rang a taxi to take me to the address. As I left my desk, my letter opener — the skean dhu — caught my eye. I grabbed it, slipped it into my raincoat pocket and dashed for the lift.

It occurs to me that I've neglected to tell you the name in the phone book, haven't I? It was Ian Thome.

chapter four

alphabetti spaghetti

THE PREVIOUS MORNING, Guy Fall had dragged himself out of bed as he did every other morning. He shared a subsiding flat at Holyrood Quadrant off Great Western Road with a fellow student with whom he was barely on speaking terms. The floral wallpaper peeled off the walls of his high-ceilinged bedroom, baring mushroom-brown damp stains. Tall, rain-pocked windows revealed the tenement's back green strewn with sodden tabloids and porno mags, orange peel, empty and open rusting tins of baked beans and chopped tomatoes and an assortment of holey supermarket polythene bags.

Chilled to the marrow, he kicked down his stale sheets and raised his head from the hollow indent of the yellowing striped pillowcase, pondering whether he was up to facing the laundrette or whether he could get away with postponing it for a further day or two. He yawned, stretched his limbs, cracking his joints, rolled himself onto his feet and stumbled off to relieve himself in the toilet, scratching his scalp, bracing himself for the arctic hall.

He lived in standard student squalor but that didn't depress him — only the laundrette, populated with its terminal captives of poverty, managed that. As a product of a middle-class suburban home located on the city's northern outskirts, Fall equated squalor with liberation. He revelled in its decadence. It was temporary poverty. It gave him a baseline from which he would chart his progress. He'd recall it with affection in years to come when he'd achieved his ambition to be the creative director in the city's hippest ad agency.

Fall was in his first year of a full-time media studies course at Glasgow University, which he was studying as a career route into advertising. Advertising was his obsession. He was as passionate about ads as other people are about books or records or films or paintings. He was a connoisseur of adverts. He could recite taglines and whistle jingles from ads he'd seen when he was three years old. Adverts were visualisations of his conception of paradise. He yearned for reality to be like an advert.

Conversely, he did all he could to avoid the news and never read a paper. If adverts were visualisations of paradise, newspapers — with their never-ending supply of fatal accidents, murders, genocidal atrocities and natural disasters — were daily confirmation of the reality of hell.

But, as Fall shuffled into the toilet and stood shivering and pissing into the lavatory whilst a tap trickled lukewarm water into a grimy bath, his romantic notions of the glamour of squalor soon evaporated.

His flatmate was a reclusive fellow student (who had never been spied on campus during daylight hours but had occasionally been sighted entering the flat from some all-nighter and heading for bed, passing Fall in the hall with a short sigh and an averted eye) with smooth white skin, whose diet seemed to consist solely of long-past-its-sell-by-date alphabetti spaghetti which, given that there had never been any evidence of used pots, pans or plates, he apparently consumed cold from the tin.

But Fall didn't pass him in the hall that morning. Instead, after crunching his way through slices of burnt toast and slurping a cup of instant coffee, he packed his bag with books and headed out for the lecture he was destined to miss.

He was destined to miss it because, as he turned to lock the flat's bottle-green storm doors behind him, a figure emerged from the shadows of the communal entrance, silenced him and dragged him back into the shadows.

chapter five

cross-reference

IT WAS THESE VERY STORM DOORS that I pounded on with the palm of my hand, having lost faith in the doorbell, early the next afternoon.

When there was still no answer, I extracted the scrap of paper once more from the breast pocket of my shirt to verify that I had the correct address. Once more, I became conscious of a distinct feeling that I was being watched. What now? Glancing at my watch, I cursed and hailed a taxi to return me to the office. I figured I'd better start editing some letters whilst I pondered my next move.

By the time I reached the office a new line of enquiry had occurred to me so that, rather than starting to edit the letters, I approached Kirsty Baird's desk instead. Kirsty Baird, you will recall, is the buxom blonde cultural commentator who happens to double up as the paper's literary editor, and she furnished me with Niamh Toe's mobile number — which meant that I was unable to deduce her place of residence from her area code — with an unsubtle wink of a mascaraed eye.

There was no reply so I left a mumbled message on the book reviewer's recall service, stressing the importance of her returning my call whilst striving not to sound overly anxious.

As I waited on tenterhooks for my phone to ring, I started to select the letters I would edit for the next morning's page with one eye on the clock and the other on the bevelled glass partition, behind which I could see the distorted bulk of John Kerr, the paper's editor, puffing away in his smoke-filled aquarium. I was wondering whether to confess to the predicament in which I found myself, his likely reaction to such a confession and its probable impact on my career prospects.

Was this not a situation that I alone had created and should accept sole responsibility for? Would not a confession equate to a pathetic attempt to shift the burden of responsibility from my own shoulders on to those of a superior? Or was a full and frank confession not my last chance of admitting my error before plunging into a labyrinth of lies from which there would be no guaranteed return?

I opted to ponder these questions further rather than act rashly, attempting, but failing, to concentrate on the letters at hand.

Half an hour later I followed Baird into the kitchen, under the pretext of rinsing my teacup, in order to interrogate her about Niamh Toe. Baird proved to be as scatty as I had suspected. It transpired that she had never actually met Toe and only ever communicated with her via her mobile. I returned to my desk no more than a minute after I'd departed it to discover that a caller had left me a voicemail. I knew before I heard her voice that it was Toe. Her message was succinct.

'Returning your call,' she drawled, sounding as if she was chewing gum. 'I'm on my way out and won't be contactable for the rest of the day. Call me now or tomorrow after twelve.'

I re-dialled her number immediately and when the ringing tone was replaced by a recording of her voice inviting me to leave a message I cursed aloud.

'Tomorrow's too late!' I blurted after the tone. 'This is urgent. Please call back.' Twenty-nine seconds later (not thirty — I counted them) my phone managed to emit a split second of a ring before I yanked the receiver from its rest.

'What's so urgent that it can't wait till tomorrow?' she asked, disinterestedly.

'I can't explain over the phone — '

'You'd better try.'

'I can't — it's a delicate matter — '

'Goodbye.'

'Ian Thome,' I said. 'I need to speak to you about Ian Thome.'

'Who's Ian Thome?'

'He wrote a letter in my paper in response to your review of a book called *Original Harm* by Tom Haine.'

'And?'

'And I really need to speak to you about it — today.'

There was a hesitation and then a sigh of exasperation.

'I'm on my way to the Mitchell Library. Meet me in the general reference section in half an hour. I'll give you five minutes.'

I arrived ten minutes early, scanned the room, but found no obvious candidates who corresponded to the voice of Niamh Toe. I endured the eternity of the next ten minutes glancing at the door, my watch and an encyclopaedia that lay open before me and within which I was attempting to appear engrossed. For the umpteenth time that day, I began to feel that I was being watched.

Two minutes later than the time allotted for our assignation, a striking girl entered. She had flawless Cadbury-coloured skin; bee-stung lips and swaying hips that she swayed straight past me and out the other door without making eye contact. Could that have been her? Should I follow her? I listened to her retreating footsteps grow faint until I substituted my doubt-filled inertia for action.

'Excuse me!' I called, my voice reverberating along the chequered tiled corridor. She stopped and glanced back to find me running towards her.

'You don't happen to be Niamh Toe, do you?' I enquired, fighting for breath.

'No,' she said, already turning away, consigning me to history with a flick of a corkscrew-curled fringe.

I stood for a moment, rooted by her rhythm, then turned heel and returned to the reference section.

On re-entering the room, I ignored the inquisitive glance from an unfamiliar librarian and, instead, carried out a rapid reconnaissance which confirmed that no new browsers had entered. Then, over in the far corner, I noticed that the entrance doors were swinging. Someone had just exited. I sprinted over, pushed them open, and scanned an empty corridor for someone who might look a likely candidate for Niamh Toe. Disconsolate, I returned to mope around until I'd convinced myself it was hopeless to wait any longer.

On my return, the librarian glanced at me again. I met her glance with a glare.

'Can I help you?' she asked.

'Not unless your name's Niamh Toe,' I said.

She gave me a look and smiled (to herself — not to me).

'You wanted to ask me something about Ian Thome,' she said.

'That's right,' I confirmed, flustered but attempting (and failing miserably) to disguise it. 'Have you read his letter in response to your review?'

'No.'

'Can I show it to you?' I asked, already retrieving it from my shirt pocket.

'No.'

'Why not?'

'I've been told it's scathing.'

'So was your review,' I said. She shrugged.

We'd reached an impasse. I seized the opportunity to assess her.

She wore no make-up. She had no need to. That said, I was intimidated more by her manner than her beauty. Though terse, I suspected that she was shielding a fragile ego. I knew all about that. She appeared incapable of penning the other letter folded in my pocket.

'Words can occasionally incite a chain reaction of excitable — even extreme — responses,' I said, alluding to the threatening letter to gauge her reaction (there wasn't one).

'Haine's book incited a strongly-worded critique from you; your critique incited a vehement defence of Haine from Ian Thome; Thome's letter incited an extreme response from somebody else — '

'Who?'

'I don't know yet — but I need to find out very quickly.'

'Why?'

I hesitated, glanced at my watch, realised that I had no time to act coy, and summarised my predicament — without revealing the precise nature of the kidnapper's demands.

'Am I a suspect?' she asked.

'Of course not,' I said.

'Why not?'

I was starting to find her directness unsettling.

'Have you ever heard of Craig Liddell?' She ignored this blatant diversionary tactic.

'Why am I not a suspect?'

'Because,' I stumbled, 'you don't look capable of such a thing.'

'Looks can be deceiving,' she said. 'What does a kidnapper look like?'

'I don't know — not like you. *Should* you be a suspect?'

'Who's Craig Liddell?' she asked, and I told her, not realising till later that she'd deployed my own diversionary tactic against me.

I explained that the letter writer was agitated about *Original Harm* and antagonistic towards its author while her book review revealed her to be a woman of conviction and wondered aloud whether she was aware of any individual or organisation whose views mirrored those expressed within the letter.

'Have you even *read Original Harm*?' she asked.

chapter six

crosswords

NIAMH TOE'S REMARK confirmed my worst fear — art was imitating life which, in turn, was imitating art. It was the conclusion I'd been trying to avoid reaching ever since I'd read the letter: the kidnapper was most likely a member of The Amino.

In *Original Harm*, The Amino is an embryonic subculture characterised by a late-teenage middle-class suburbanite reaction to the liberal values held by its parents. It's a group of extremist ascetics most easily identified by their negativity — anti-drink, anti-drug, anti-promiscuity, anti-abortion, anti-homosexuality, anti-atheism — whose underlying philosophy could most easily be summarised as anti-tolerant. In *Original Harm* The Amino had taken its new Puritanism to its illogical conclusion by seeking to enforce it through escalating acts of violence and terrorism.

But whilst *Original Harm* was based on fact, it was, nevertheless, a work of fiction, and I knew that The Amino was fictitious; or at least it had been (and I did do) — until then.

A glance at my watch threw me into a panic and I rushed back to the office to find that the afternoon mail had arrived, replenishing my never-ending supply of letters. In a state of consternation, I set off for the kitchen to brew myself a cup of peppermint tea to try to contrive some semblance of composure, gather my thoughts and determine a course of action which would somehow solve the dilemma I'd unwittingly designed for myself to stumble into.

I noticed the paper's freelance crossword compiler sitting in a corner of the kitchen playing Scrabble by himself. Chris (I didn't know his surname, he was only ever known as 'Chris the Crossword Compiler') invited me to join him in a game. When I declined, I must have pierced myself with a pang of guilt at the thought that I might have affronted him; at least that's the only reason I can think why I proceeded to confide in him.

I heaved a sigh and told him all about the anonymous letter; reminded him of the cruel fate that had befallen Craig Liddell; summarised the contents of Niamh Toe's book review and Ian Thorne's letter I'd published by way of response; outlined the plot of Tom Haine's *Original Harm*; told him how I'd discovered Ian Thorne's number and address in the phone book but had been unable to make contact with him, though I subsequently *had* been able to make contact with Niamh Toe, who seemed to suggest that the key to deciphering the identity of the letter writer could be found in *Original Harm* and that he was most likely a member of a fictitious organisation called The Amino. When I'd finished, I asked him what I should do about the letter.

'You must ask Kerr to print it on tomorrow's front page,' he said.

'Wouldn't that be succumbing to blackmail?'

'It's not your responsibility,' he insisted. 'The alternative is blood on your hands.'

I sighed. He was simply articulating what I already knew but, of course, I hadn't told him the whole story. I had my reasons for not running to Kerr straight away. It *was* my responsibility. I thanked him for his advice and started to head for my desk.

'I wonder,' commented Chris, 'if it's merely coincidence that all the names of the characters in your little story — with the exception of Craig Liddell — are anagrams of "I am not he"?'

This observation was, of course, no mere insignificant coincidence, and, whilst it caught me off guard, it didn't come as a complete surprise — for reasons that, if you haven't already guessed by now, are about to become clear.

Let me explain.

As you know, there's never any shortage of letters for me to edit. Even so, a couple of days before that fateful morning, I'd succumbed to a long suppressed desire to be a letter *writer* rather than a letter *editor* (there are participants and spectators in life, writers and readers, and, while I'd almost resigned myself to the fact that I belonged to the latter categories, I'd always wanted to pluck up the courage and at least have a stab at breaking through to the former) so that, for the first and last time, I wrote a letter myself, under the pseudonym Ian Thome. It never occurred to me that there would be such an overreaction to it or that there might be a real Ian Thome who would become implicated.

But that doesn't really explain why I chose to publish the particular letter I did.

Whilst I was obviously unsurprised by Chris the Crossword Compiler's observation that the name Ian Thome was an anagram of 'I am not he', I was also unsurprised by his observation that the name Tom Haine was a variation of the same anagrammatic pseudonym — because I am also the author of *Original Harm*.

I published my debut novel under a pseudonym for a number of reasons, partly to deflect any forthcoming adverse criticism directed at myself, but — in an admittedly shocking example of double standards — I made my pseudonym an anagram of 'I am not he' because my vanity meant that, in the event of a *favourable* critical reception, I wanted readers to realise that Tom Haine was a pseudonym and to become intrigued about, and perhaps proceed to decipher, my real identity.

When Niamh Toe's scathing review appeared in the pages of my own paper, confirming my fear of being subjected to ridicule,

I succumbed to the temptation to defend myself (under the guise of the pseudonym Ian Thome — why I chose to employ an anagrammatic variation of the pseudonym under which I published the book I can't easily explain) by publishing a letter full of praise for myself.

But this is where Chris the Crossword Compiler's observation really did surprise me. It hadn't occurred to me that the name Niamh Toe was also an anagram of 'I am not he'. What could this mean? I couldn't begin to hazard a guess and so it was with a sense of unease that I reread the anonymous letter in an attempt to make some sense of it all.

Then, when I reread the reference to Craig Liddell's murder, I realised that Toni Mahe — the name of the mysterious hotel guest and prime suspect of his murder — was *also* an anagram of 'I am not he'. This realisation more than surprised me; it more than disturbed me — it *terrified* me.

chapter seven

filling empty space

IT WAS WITH A SENSE OF TREPIDATION that I returned to my desk and attempted to refocus my attention on the editing of the letters. I was now convinced that I'd unwittingly put some unsuspecting innocent called Ian Thome's life at risk and — more to the point — had placed myself in a perilous position too. What was I to do?

For the remainder of the afternoon I swayed between the two options which presented themselves to me: confess all to Kerr, spout contrition and beg for forgiveness; or take the incriminating evidence of the letter into a toilet cubicle, tear it to shreds, throw it into the lavatory, piss on it and flush it out of my life with a view to denying all knowledge of its existence should its author ever feel obliged to demonstrate his sincerity and fulfil his threat.

On several occasions I found myself approaching either Kerr's office or the toilet before returning to my desk to fret further on the matter until, finally, a third way occurred to me; a compromise lurking somewhere in the sprawling expanse separating confession from denial.

I approached Kerr's smoke-filled aquarium and, after an interminable pause pregnant with wavering resolve, knocked on his door. He bade me enter with a gruff command and, through the swirling clouds, the impatience of his glare demanded I justify my intrusion.

I approached his desk, proffering the crumpled letter in my outstretched hand.

'I don't know whether this is from a crank or what,' I said, attempting to sound unconcerned and conscientious, breathing shallowly in a forlorn attempt at minimising the damaging effect of passive smoke inhalation, 'but I thought I'd better run it past you, just to be on the safe side.'

'What is it?' he barked, regarding the letter where it lay with disdain.

'It's a letter,' I said.

'I can see that,' he snapped before being convulsed by a dry coughing fit. 'Why have you brought it to me?'

I sighed. I'd much rather he'd read it for himself. Now I'd have to explain its contents to him. I did so as concisely as I could.

'When did you receive it?'

'Just now,' I lied.

He looked at his watch.

'Fuck this,' he said, sighing to himself. I shrugged and also sighed in a half-hearted attempt at empathy.

My strategy, my third way, it will now have become clear, involved passing the burden of responsibility over to my editor whilst simultaneously seeking to conceal the extent of my own duplicitous role as the unwitting architect of the predicament. It was a risky strategy, of that there was no doubt, but, so far as I could fathom, its failure would leave me occupying a position no worse than either of the alternative avenues open to me so that, at the very least, it might buy me some time.

Kerr grabbed a phone and lit a cigarette, sucking on it for dear death as he dialled.

'Who're you calling?' I asked, wondering if he'd already made a decision on whether or not to contact the police and, if so, how

I felt about it — it was a decision I'd been avoiding making since receipt of the letter.

'Findlay,' he barked. Bill Findlay was the paper's managing director and Kerr's closest link to the board of directors. My newspaper was only one of a portfolio of media titles, comprising an evening tabloid, a sister Sunday, a magazine division and significant stakes in local television and radio stations, owned by the company.

Kerr looked up at me. 'We're going to have to call an emergency meeting — and you'll be attending.'

He addressed me in such a disgruntled fashion and with such an accusatory tone that, if I hadn't been absolutely positive that there was no way that he could have known that I was responsible for the predicament in which he now found himself, I would have been convinced that he knew that I was.

Whilst I had been aware that I no longer had the option of destroying the letter and denying all knowledge of its existence, it was only now that I realised that it was also too late for me to proffer a full and frank confession. I'd embarked upon the third way and there was now no alternative but to proceed.

A few moments later, Kerr's impeccably power-dressed PA was summoned into the aquarium to transform barked orders into immediate administrative action. Kerr exited his aquarium and strode to the lift. We stepped out onto the top floor to find that the board had already convened in the opulent oak-panelled boardroom.

If I was intimidated by Kerr's PA then I was overwhelmed by the almost palpable power and impenetrable sense of self-worth emanating from the stern-faced, middle-aged, middle class men who constituted the board of directors. Their grudging tolerance of Kerr and refusal to acknowledge my own presence presented me with an enlightened perspective of the paper's hierarchy and I realised that, for all the years I'd been there and fancied that I'd become a vital component of an organisation, the operation of which I felt I had an implicit understanding as a consequence of years of daily experience, I remained no more than an overhead that could be dismissed and replaced on a whim with no necessity for deliberation and no perceived detrimental consequence worthy of consideration.

I had a sudden insight that the board of directors' entire perception of the paper was the exact opposite of my own in that, whilst for me adverts were what got in the way of editorial, so far as the board was concerned, editorial was the stuff that filled the empty space around the ads. The difference in our respective perspectives was that fundamental and, once I realised it, I found it hard to believe that I'd been oblivious to it all these years. I thought of a new pseudonym for myself: Phil Space — but by now it was too late.

Kerr's PA slipped into the room and handed him copies of the letter. The board members took their seats around the mahogany table as a hidden door in the oak panelling opened on the far side of the room. A white-whiskered man shuffled into the room and slumped in the nearest chair. I noticed a discreet flesh-coloured hearing aid protruding from his left ear. The murmuring had concluded on his entrance.

At the other end of the table Findlay cleared his throat, thanked the board members for their presence and invited Kerr to summarise the situation. Kerr indulged himself with the briefest glance of disgust in my direction (a glance made not only to underline to me — but also to signal to his attentive audience — that he held me directly responsible for the predicament within which he now found himself) before rising to distribute copies of the letter around the table, starting with White Whiskers. As he did so, he said, 'Gentlemen, the letter you have before you was received by our letters page editor' — here he nodded to me — 'no more than five minutes ago. As you can see, it's a quite blatant attempt by an apparently dangerous extremist to force us into publicising his point of view. I've called this meeting to determine collectively an appropriate response. Firstly, we have to decide whether or not to take its threats seriously — '

'Given the reference to Craig Liddell, I don't see how we can afford not to,' mumbled White Whiskers.

'That being so,' proceeded Kerr, irritated by this interruption, 'so far as I can see, we're faced with two options: either we meet the demands as set out in the letter, thereby forfeiting the very foundation on which this paper was founded — the right of free speech — and laying ourselves open to future copycat threats in the hope that we save the life of the hostage; or, alternatively, we refuse point-blank to meet the demands as set out in the letter and, instead, contact the police — a course of action which would uphold our principles and safeguard us against any future copycat threats, but might have a fatal consequence for the hostage.'

'Which option do you propose?' enquired White Whiskers. Kerr stalled and surveyed the room, seeking clues to help him gauge the mood of the board. They remained inscrutable. On impulse I decided to try and bail him out.

'There might be a third way,' I suggested. The glower Kerr bestowed on me showed that he was entirely unappreciative of my intervention (it reminded me why some of his staff, emboldened by a dram or two after hours in the Space Bar would, on occasion, substitute his Christian name for its Spanish equivalent 'Juan' — behind his back, of course. Indeed 'Juan' had become Kerr's unofficial nickname — the juvenile humour behind it only making sense to those who knew his surname). It was a glower reproduced by the board of directors, all of whom appeared outraged that I should have the impertinence to speak without having first been spoken to.

'And what would that be?' enquired White Whiskers, cupping his hand to his ear. I cleared my throat and spoke louder than I normally would.

'To run the letter on the front page, unedited as demanded, but to surround it with editorial condemning it outright and

34

defending the right of free speech. It seems to me that, whilst the letter is an outright threat, it also presents us with an opportunity — '

'How so?' interrupted Findlay.

'It presents us with an opportunity to exploit an exclusive (no one else knows about the letter) from the inside — '

' — I could run the story on our morning news bulletin,' proposed an unidentified board member, as if it was his idea.

'I could use it on our evening news programme,' suggested another.

'We could get our investigative team onto it,' added Findlay. 'Find out exactly what prompted this letter; start a search for the kidnapper — it's obviously the same guy who murdered Liddell.'

'Can you do all that for tomorrow's edition?' enquired White Whiskers. Findlay assured him that he could, before looking towards Kerr for confirmation. 'Good. Let's get to it, gentlemen.'

As the room began to empty, Whiskers indicated to Findlay to remain seated. Only once they were alone did he turn to him and, in a confidential tone, instruct him to make contact with 'our friend, the Chief Constable' on the QT to put him in the picture and seek his advice about how best to proceed without alerting the kidnapper to the fact that they'd made contact.

'And while you're at it, make contact with that private eye working on the Liddell murder investigation. What's her name again?'

'Pardos,' said Findlay.

'That's right,' said Whiskers. 'But don't, for God's sake, let her know that we've tipped off the Chief Constable and, more importantly, don't let *him* know about *her*.'

Once I'd finished editing the letters and passed them to the sub-editor to lay out, I left the small matter of the front page to the reporters and slipped out into the evening drizzle where, instead of heading for the bus stop, which was my usual routine, I returned to the Mitchell.

As I suspected, Niamh Toe, or whatever her real name was, was nowhere to be found. Even if she was a bona fide librarian — and I had my doubts — then the chances were that her shift had finished. Nevertheless, I decided to enquire about her whereabouts on the off chance that someone could enlighten me.

Needless to say, the surly librarian on duty had never heard of a Niamh Toe nor knew of any staff member fitting her description.

PART TWO

atone him

chapter eight

flesh out

THAT NIGHT, as I teetered on the brink of sleep, I plunged into an abyss and was jolted fully awake by an involuntary jerk.

The first time this had happened to me was on holiday in Majorca years ago; the first night I'd gone to bed without Lisa to wrap myself around. I remember I'd got up and stumbled through to Andy's room to snuggle in to him instead. The second time, the following night, I once again stumbled through to Andy's room, only to be confronted by an empty bed. When the plunge into the abyss became a nightly occurrence, the doctor prescribed a course of sedatives, but an instinctive need to plumb the depths of suffering left me immune to the temptation to dull its intensity, and I took to wandering the streets instead.

The other night, because the plunge had reprised itself, I decided to resurrect the early hours street walk.

At night, city streets, lit by starburst orange-haloed lampposts, are deserted.

Late-night wandering can foster doodles of wondering which, occasionally, help put pressing concerns into perspective; stripping layers of trivia from long-forgotten fundamental truths. On such occasions, blind to my surroundings, submerged in reveries of halcyon days with Lisa and Andy, I'd emerge to find myself in unfamiliar districts and it would take an angst-ridden hour or longer to discover the reassurance of a familiar vicinity from which I could thread my way home; or else I'd emerge to find myself haunting a nondescript place around which the passage of time had woven an intricate pattern of poignancy; a particular bus stop or former friend's flat or a favourite pub. I remember once emerging before my primary school, unable to drag myself from the gates, gazing through the railings into the small, square concrete playground, hearing the raucous joy of kids playing echoing around the empty yard with a loud and limitless energy for life fuelled by a concrete optimism without trace of the faintest hairline fracture of self-doubt.

The other night, fear swamped by reflection, I entered Queen's Park, an oasis of darkness in the lamppost-lit cityscape, acknowledging a frisson of danger, alert and surveying the shadowy surroundings. I hesitated to ponder the duck pond: the sleeping swans, beaks tucked tightly beneath wings; the drowned upturned shopping trolley adorned with strands of ASDA carrier bags billowing in the breeze; the oily, stagnant water choking on rusted and crushed cans of Tennent's lager, spawny condoms and cigarette stubs; the moon-glinted, shattered-glass-spangled tarmac rimming the pool spattered with blobs of bird shit from the flocks of pigeons and seagulls that scavenged the bread crusts brought for the ducks by Sunday-afternoon parents doting on runny-nosed, ruddy-cheeked, mini Michelin-man toddlers.

I passed by the locked, vandalised amphitheatre and wandered up a steep path, noticing a broad tree-lined avenue slope down to grand, gilded gates and out on to Victoria Road, which forged straight on into the heart of the city and beyond to the horizon where, on a clear day, you could see the snow-peaked Campsies.

I proceeded to the flagpole at the summit where, perched on a bench buffeted by the wind, I surveyed the city that circled below me.

I was reminiscing about an evening in Majorca's Port de Soller with Lisa when, in a post-coital bliss, we lounged, still naked, on the veranda of our rented villa toking a joint and sipping sangria, listening to Jobim, inhaling the fragrance from the rampant bougainvillaea amongst the cluster of cypress trees.

We'd hired a moped that morning and snaked our way up over the winding mountain road to Deia, where we bumped down a dirt track to the cove and found a small café, signalled by a cluster of faded, striped sun umbrellas, perched on the edge of a promontory overlooking the bay. We slaked our thirst with Cokes and Sprites and San Miguels. We donned shades, balmed lips, dipped into sandy paperbacks, massaged each other with coconut-scented sun cream and dived into the crests of waves to bathe our burning bodies in the sun-kissed sea.

I had interrupted the post-coital reverie to pen postcards, a signal for Lisa to retreat behind the pages of her book. Lisa was an avid reader. She devoured books and they consumed her. I understand now that I was jealous of her books: jealous because they satisfied a need I couldn't; jealous of their ability to enrapture her; jealous of the time she devoted to them; jealous because they stole her away from me.

'Is a life spent reading worth living?' I'd once asked.

She'd shrugged and, only half-joking, said, 'Two things make life worth living: sex and books.'

That night she fucked me while finishing off George Bataille's *Story of the Eye*.

Lisa always read but she never wrote. She never sent postcards or birthday cards or Valentine cards or letters. I always sent them to her and she always thanked me for them. It took me longer than it should have to learn not to comment on her lack of reciprocation.

The first letter she wrote me was the last letter she wrote me.

She said that she never sent postcards because she felt incapable of compressing a week or more of novel experiences into a sentence or two. She said that she never sent a birthday card because the passage of time, being beyond control, wasn't an achievement and so wasn't a cause for celebration. She said that she never sent Valentine cards because the words inside them bore no relation to how she felt and, anyway, she didn't *know* how she felt. And if she did, she couldn't write it. And if she could, she wouldn't. She said that she never sent letters because she didn't believe that anyone could express themselves accurately through writing. She argued that words are spoken and then remembered or forgotten, depending on memory, which edits what it considers to be important, whilst time distorts the importance of written words by eroding the context within which they were written.

She never said, 'I love you', but I know that she did.

'I can tell you that I love you without opening my mouth,' she said. 'Words aren't necessary. You get the message. Language lets us down. It's hard enough trying to articulate things without trying to write about them. Words can't express how I feel. I'm lost for words. I'm speechless. You can't write in clichés but everyone talks in clichés. Actions speak louder than words,' she said, pushing my head down between her legs.

But I loved writing and receiving letters. I'd exchanged letters on a monthly basis with a pen-pal called Liam who lived in Brooklyn, New York, (I'd made contact with him through an international reading club — in the days when I devoured books as avidly as Lisa does now), from when I was old enough to write and post them on my own until shortly after I met Lisa, who found this a constant source of amusement.

'Whatever do you find to write about?' she'd ridicule and I'd embark on a stumbling self-conscious self-analysis of my motivations, trying to explain that how, on reflection, I could see that I used Liam as a confidant because the distance somehow made it easier to express all the things that mattered, all the things that you withheld from everyone else for fear of reprisals — only to stop mid-sentence when I noticed her smirk.

'What things?' she goaded.

'I don't know,' I shrugged. 'Things. I don't remember.' Utterly humiliated by Lisa's mocking, I vowed there and then to bring my long-standing epistolary friendship with Liam to an abrupt conclusion.

'Did you ever meet?' she asked and, annoyed by her tone, I changed the subject.

I sent her birthday cards and Valentine cards every year. When she became a mother, I sent her Mother's Day cards. When she fell ill, I sent her Get Well Soon cards. One year, aggrieved at yet again not receiving a birthday card from her, despite the dropping of heavy hints, I decided not to send her one. She sulked the entire evening, refusing to confess the cause of her foul temper, but I knew. I knew too to let it be. An unspoken rule of our relationship, drawn up in its infancy, was that she was permitted to ridicule me, as freely and as frequently as she saw fit, but on no account was I ever allowed to taunt her.

She lay there on the inflatable blue-bottomed dinghy out on the veranda, her head propped up against the bow; her face hidden behind the pages of her book, gobbling a peach, its juice dribbling down her chin; her crossed ankles resting on the stern; her crucifix nestling in the valley of her breasts, glinting in the sunshine; her straw-coloured hair which, when I twirled it around my index finger, looked like string... and I inhaled her. She smelled of summer.

I was stirred from my reverie by a shiver. Turning up the collar of my jacket, I dug my hands deeper into its pockets, surveying the cityscape once more, noticing the steeples piercing the dawn sky, like a cluster of cold, concrete cypress trees.

'Do you approve of abortion?' she'd asked. Just like that. I remember it distinctly. She caught me unawares. We were planting herbs in the back green under the low grey clouds of an oppressive Sunday afternoon. She didn't stop what she was

43

doing, digging pockets in the earth with a trowel into which she buried the roots of mint and parsley and sage, or look to gauge my reaction.

'I think it's every woman's right,' I said. I was about to enquire why she'd asked when she snorted and shook her head. I waited for her to confirm my suspicions. I waited for an opportunity to burst into celebration at the miracle of creation. I waited while she pressed rosemary into the earth. I waited.

Then, aware of the scent of thyme on my hands, I said, 'But I don't want you to have an abortion,' and wandered in to the kitchen to wash it away.

I cut to the baby crying in his cot in the dead of night. Lisa was sound asleep. I dragged myself out of bed to feed him. Stumbling in the dark, I lifted him and, finding that he was wet, washed, dried, talcummed and changed him. Then I heated up his formula milk in the microwave (Lisa had persevered with breast feeding for seven raw and cracked days before dispatching me to Boots with precise instructions to procure the correct formula, brand and quantity of artificial milk) and, sitting in the splintered cane rocking chair, bought from an auction a few months earlier specifically for this purpose, rocked and hummed *Hush a Bye Baby* and fed him and dozed, being intermittently woken by cars driving along the wet road and over the loose drain at the T-junction — the two syllable metallic ca-clunk as the front, then the rear, passenger-side wheels drove over the slack metal lid. I can hear it even now. Ca-clunk.

Awakening again, I listened to the wind howling and, as I cradled my newborn son in my arms and watched Lisa sleeping, her mouth slack, her breathing heavy, realised I was adrift and alone.

Lisa had grown weary. Too tired to rise in the morning. Too tired to stay awake in the evening. She'd fallen into the habit of slumping in front of the television, swamped by lethargy, with Andy (we'd baptised the baby Andrew after Lisa's dad; the dad who'd abandoned her mum and herself before she was old enough to remember him) wreaking havoc around her. I had assumed her fatigue to be a temporary reaction to the strains of labour and the stresses of motherhood, but the languorous days soon became weeks before stretching out into months and, eventually, years.

When she became too tired to read and too tired to fuck I knew something, somewhere had gone awry.

At weekends I'd leave her to watch her television in peace and quiet and take Andy to the park to play. It was me who taught him how to walk. It was me who taught him how to wipe his bottom and flush the toilet and wash his hands. It was me who taught him how to use a knife and fork. It was me who taught him how to swim. It was me who taught him how to ride his bike, to fly a kite and to tie his shoelaces. It was me whom he read his homework to and it was me who helped him hone his handwriting. This was probably my proudest achievement. His calligraphy was an aesthetic delight: his O's were perfectly round; his I's tall and straight; his S's satisfyingly symmetrical — I could go on through the whole alphabet.

If she had had the patience or the perseverance or the energy, Lisa would have taught him her faith.

Between the opposite banks of faith and faithlessness our relationship coursed like a polluted river whose toxic undercurrents neither dared probe. Having grown to accept that the banks could not be bridged, we agreed to keep our own counsel with regard to our fundamental disparity so that, whilst her faith and my faithlessness remained an implicit understanding, it was in both our interests not to strain the sturdiness of that understanding by forcing it into a position whereby it was made explicit — until Andy arrived and I insisted on resisting Lisa's persistent attempts at infantile indoctrination.

Whilst I despised her faith, I knew too that Andy owed his life to it. Without it, she'd have had an abortion, whatever my thoughts on the matter might have been. This realisation was an important impetus behind *Original Harm*.

More specifically, *Original Harm* had been prompted by a news item on the murder of a doctor en route to witness the birth of his son. Because the doctor had performed a number of terminations, a pro-life group had claimed responsibility for his death.

Since I'd become a father, I'd become increasingly sensitive to news of murders and atrocities and tragedies, particularly where children were concerned. I found that I would rather switch off the television or turn the page than be exposed to this reality. The frequency and horror of such incidents seemed to me to demand urgent investigation. I fancied that, by detailed consideration of the murder of the doctor, I might be able to expose some common factors underlying such atrocities that could perhaps help me understand what motivates their perpetrators.

That was one reason why I started writing, but perhaps a more fundamental reason was selfishness. Writing fulfilled a need to do something more productive with my time than while it away in passive consumption like Lisa. Part of me despised Lisa for what she was doing to herself. I couldn't understand it. That she didn't love herself any more seemed obvious. That she didn't love me any more I could learn to live with. But that she didn't love Andy was incomprehensible. Yet what other conclusion could I reach when she would rather watch an episode of *EastEnders* than read him a story in bed?

Another motivation for my writing was my jealousy of the authors who had so captivated Lisa. I needed to possess her totally and conceived the notion that this was possible only if it was *my* writing in which she was immersed. I needed to enrapture her through my words. I needed to possess her imagination as much as her flesh. I needed her to need me for the words I'd written as much as for who she knew me to be.

I'd also intended that writing would help preserve precious memories but, in fact, I realised, too late, that, instead of preserving memory, writing distorted it so that, when I reread something I'd written some time previously, the boundary between fact and fiction had become blurred to a degree where I became uncertain of my memory. The memories I'd used as a starting point for my writing had been deliberately distorted — biographical facts fabricated, exaggerated and dramatised — and these fictionalised memories had, through the process of writing about them, superseded the real memories so that, in retrospect, I was left floundering in an indistinct factional world.

As Lisa spent each evening slumped before a stream of soaps and repeated, canned-laughtered 1970s sitcoms which she'd first watched in her early teens, I'd tuck in Andy and kiss him goodnight, then retire to the kitchen to wash and dry the dishes before sitting at the unsteady table to write.

I wrote aimlessly at first. I had no deadline and so I took my time. I took my time because another motive for writing was to fill time.

And I watched in wonder as Andy grew from a chubby baby into a toddler, stretching into a cherubic wee boy with a cowlick, missing front teeth and a dimpled grin that placed all the anxieties of my stalled career into perspective. My parents and Lisa's mum all agreed that Andy was a miniature version of Lisa.

Why is the sky blue? What's love? What's death? Why do people kill other people? Where was I before I was born? What's God? My inadequate replies to his infinite supply of questions only prompted further questions and revealed to me the extent of my own ignorance.

When Andy was seven he still looked like a mini version of his mum but, sometimes, I recognised my own voice spilling from his lips, my own slant on things revealed through incidental comments suggesting that, inside, he was more a mini version of me. Whilst I'd purposely taught him the necessary skills required for socialisation, he'd incidentally been imbued with many of my perspectives. This paternal influence did not pass unnoticed by Lisa, who contradicted any exceptionable opinion she felt Andy had inherited from me.

Most notably, the matter of his faith became one of the last major battles in our internecine warfare for control over Andy before, like all the previous battles, it was consigned to the burgeoning list of taboos that plunged any conversation surviving between us into the necessary trivialities. Hostilities were settled by a compromise package thrashed out over a series of summit meetings between Andy's grannies — who despised each other and struggled to hide their mutual loathing whenever they were in his presence — which involved Andy attending a non-denominational school provided that he would accompany Lisa to Mass on Sundays.

I agreed to this concession for two reasons. Firstly, despite my atheism, I was willing to accept (though I would never admit as much to Lisa) that, theoretically, faith could provide a degree of comfort when encountering death; it could act as a crutch which Andy could lean on until such time as he recognised religion for the superstitious mumbo jumbo that it was, when he could discard it and join me in faithlessness.

Secondly, I suspected, accurately in retrospect, that Lisa's lethargy would lead to a steady decline in her attendance at Mass.

One of the paternal influences that Lisa had either been unwilling or unable to unravel was that Andy had inherited my love for writing. At my suggestion, at the age of seven, he'd embarked on a regular correspondence with a pen-pal, sourced through an international reading club, just as I had done before him. Where we differed, though, was that my pen-pal was a boy whilst Andy's was a girl. You were the same age as him and you lived in Vancouver. That was all he would tell me about you. He was secretive in his correspondence and I respected his privacy. I remembered how precious my privacy was to me at his age and so, whilst I had ample opportunity to rifle through the not-very-well-hidden 'secret' box where he stored his correspondence, I was never tempted to do so.

We took Andy on his first foreign holiday that same year, to Majorca, Port de Soller, where Lisa and I had visited some years earlier. I made all the arrangements as Lisa's chronic fatigue had reduced her existence to one long, interminable yawn. I viewed the holiday as a last-ditch attempt to reawaken memories of happier times. I thought that perhaps memories and sunshine and sea air might reinvigorate her. In retrospect I realise how naive a notion that had been. But I was desperate. Needless to say, the holiday didn't transpire quite as I had envisaged it.

Although I booked the exact same apartment with the exact same veranda, and although the sight of the cluster of cypress trees and bougainvillaea after all this time *did* rekindle a long-extinguished fire within me, it was but a flickering flame instantly snuffed out by Lisa's habitual heaved sigh of despondency.

We lounged out on the veranda, but not in the state of post-coital bliss of my treasured memory — coitus and bliss had long been conspicuous by their absence. It was Andy who now lounged naked on a dinghy, gobbling peaches and penning postcards whilst Lisa, miserable without her daily diet of soaps and quiz shows, moped in the shade and refused to come down to the beach because she'd developed an aversion to sand, and so I resigned myself to the futility of my hopes of resurrection of happier times.

At seven o'clock on the seventh morning, the first day of our second week, I was woken by a knock at the door. Startled, I verified that Andy was still asleep and, since Lisa hadn't rushed to answer the door, surmised that she must be behind it, no doubt returning from one of her irregular but not infrequent insomnia-inspired dawn jaunts. Instead, I opened the door to find an officious policeman with military bearing dressed in an immaculate uniform. He bowed curtly, removed his helmet and offered me

49

an item of jewellery. I lifted it from his palm and examined it. It was a crucifix. I shrugged and waited for an explanation.

'You recognise it — yes?' he prompted, in stilted English.

'My wife has one similar,' I commented, still not understanding the connection. He waited until I did.

Despite a prolonged, wandering circumnavigation, frequently interrupted by profuse and quite unnecessary apologies for his faltering English, the policeman eventually arrived at the purpose of his early morning visitation and informed me that Lisa's body had been discovered by a couple of fishermen at the harbour earlier that morning. After expressing his condolences, he crossed himself, whispered a blessing in Catalan and told me that procedure required that I formally identify her body. He also suggested that, should I feel up to it, I could help him in his enquiry into the events leading up to her death. Although there was no trace of suspicion in his tone, I was engulfed by guilt and, imagining myself as the prime suspect in a murder investigation, I explained that my son was still sound asleep — and I found myself moving aside to show him Andy sleeping on the fold-down settee for fear that he should think I was lying and seeking instead to buy myself some time to devise a desperate getaway — and so he arranged to return later that morning.

As he turned to leave, I heard myself wondering aloud how he'd known to come to this apartment and he told me that the key to the apartment had been found 'on the body'. I felt foolish for thinking about, but not thinking through, such a triviality, but the finality of the phrase 'on the body' forced me to visualise Lisa's drowned corpse.

Realising that I still held Lisa's crucifix in my scrunched-up fist, I hung it around my neck. Wondering how I felt about the policeman's news, I searched the bathroom cabinet for the box of paracetamol I'd bought at the airport in anticipation of a holiday hangover and, when I couldn't find it, ransacked the apartment for the still-unopened bottle of duty-free Macallan to pour myself a stiff measure. I never found it. The next day the post-mortem would reveal that, at the time of her death, Lisa had had enough paracetamol and alcohol in her bloodstream to intoxicate her. The cause of death was confirmed as drowning and it was postulated that, in a drunken stupor, she'd stumbled off the pier and into the sea.

My ransacking of the apartment might have failed to unearth the whisky, but I did discover an unfolded letter on the bedside table. Dated the day before, and written with what looked like a blunt eyeliner pencil, I didn't recognise the cramped handwriting but I did recognise Lisa's signature. I'll reproduce it for you verbatim. I wouldn't know how else to relate its contents to you.

Morgan and Andy,

I betrayed your faith. I took your love and never returned it. I am faithless. You're better off without me. Forget about me. Nothing matters to me. Not even you. Nothing.

Lisa

Following the realisation that I'd discovered Lisa's suicide note; I was intrigued then perplexed by its content. Though terse, it seemed to me to be open to misinterpretation. What did she mean, for example, by 'I betrayed your faith'? Did she simply mean, as suggested by the following sentence, that she betrayed us (the letter was clearly directed to both me and Andy) through her inability to reciprocate our love, or was she, perhaps, referring to something more specific and, if so, what exactly? And what of 'I am faithless'? Did this mean that, ultimately, she had traversed the polluted river that separated us and had accepted the absurdity of her faith and, if so, was it possible that the stark perspective she perceived from my side of the riverbank had led her to take her own life? Such a notion led me to accuse myself of culpability and shoot a quiver of guilt-tipped arrows into my own heart. And how could she possibly write 'Nothing matters to me. Not even you' to her son? She could write that to me, if that was a true reflection of how she felt, which I didn't believe, but how could she write that to Andy? Could she *really* have intended the last message to her son to be an unequivocal denial of her love for him? Perhaps the letter wasn't a suicide note after all ... perhaps it was only a discarded draft of passing thoughts that she'd intended to destroy and was never meant to have been read. She loved me and she loved Andy — whatever she'd written. How could she write 'Nothing matters' when everything matters? Everything! Was I reading too much into something that had been scribbled by someone who'd just decided to kill herself? Had her words been carefully chosen or were they a spontaneous outburst? Why did that matter? Because it determined how to interpret the letter. If the letter *was* a genuine suicide note, then perhaps its last sentences were a reverse expression of her true feelings, which she was seeking to deny in the hope that we, Andy and myself, would accept them at face value and, beyond our immediate distress, find it easier to continue without her — so that when she wrote 'Nothing matters to me. Not even you', what she really meant was 'Everything matters to me. Especially you.' Or was my failure to accept her at her word merely evidence of my inability to comprehend her?

I reread the letter one last time, committed it to memory, then lit it and watched it burn.

I chose to burn it, firstly, and most importantly, because I wanted to shield Andy from ever discovering that his mother had been a suicide — I could only envisage such knowledge having a damaging effect — and, secondly, because I had a notion that, if it were to discover that Lisa had taken her own life, her Church might prove reticent to perform a full funeral and, inexplicable even to myself, I'd decided that, although, or maybe because, I saw it as the source of all our enmity, I wanted to make a reconciliatory gesture — albeit posthumous and, therefore, of symbolic value only — towards her faith.

I became conscious of Andy snoring, curled like a foetus, drool dribbling from his slack mouth, sound in the unquestioning trust in the love and infallibility of his parents and certainty of his security; a certainty which a truth, however whispered, would bludgeon; and, for the first time, I realised that there was a time and a place for well-intentioned lies; that fiction held a valid function; that innocence must be prolonged for as long as possible and that I had to enact a delicate damage-limitation exercise by couching the truth in the language of faith.

Later, when he'd woken, I waited for him to ask me the inevitable question. Mercifully, I didn't have to wait long.

'Where's Mummy?' he asked, still yawning, no trace of concern in his voice.

I told him that she'd gone away and wouldn't be coming back. I told him that God had come for her during the night and taken her with Him to heaven while he was asleep. I told him that she was very sad to have had to leave him without saying goodbye. I told him that she had become an angel in heaven and would be looking down on him at this very moment. I told him that she had told me to tell him not to be sad because she was happy. I told him that she had given me her crucifix to give to him and I took it from my neck and I put it over his and, as I did so, I told him that she'd told me to tell him that she loved him.

'Will I see Mummy when it's time for *me* to go to heaven?' he asked.

'Perhaps,' I said, 'perhaps. But that won't be for a long, long time.'

Then, to distract him, I took him shopping for a present. He chose a fishing net and we wandered down to the harbour. He showed no signs of grief. I treated him to his favourite strawberry ice-lolly on the way. It soon occurred to me that we were fishing in the vicinity where Lisa's body had been found. Unable to conjure a valid reason for delaying further my appointment at the police station, I resigned myself to confronting my dread.

53

A policewoman distracted Andy with a colouring book and crayons while the policeman who'd woken me that morning led me to the nearby morgue.

I'd never seen a dead body before but I'd seen the scene on television on several occasions, which must account for the fact that, as I entered the mortuary, I felt disembodied, unsure of how to act or react, as if I was watching myself on television.

On a stainless steel trolley, beneath a starched white creased sheet, lay the outline of a body. Its splayed feet made a long, thin, triangular valley of shadow where a depression descended into the hollow between its legs, coming to a point at its crotch. I recognised the shape. I had lain beside it for many years. The mortician, a girl much too young to possibly be a mortician (clearly miscast), folded back the sheet to reveal Lisa's face. I glanced at it and, after a moment's hesitation (she did not look herself — there was a huge discoloured bruise that had mushroomed over her forehead which, the mortician explained, had most likely been caused when she'd fallen into the sea and bashed it against a rock), confirmed its identity and strode from the room. After formal identification, I signed a form and was told that a post-mortem examination would now be performed to establish the exact cause of death.

My next task was to inform Lisa's mum of her death. Fairy tales weren't going to work this time. There was nothing to do but tell her the truth. I dreaded her reaction to the news — and the inevitable waves of sympathy and grief which, although I'd only started to anticipate, were already threatening to swamp me. When it occurred to me that I would have to discuss funeral arrangements with her mum, I cursed Lisa for subjecting me to this ordeal and, momentarily, and for the first time, found myself wondering whether she hadn't loved us after all.

I sleepwalked through the remainder of the day, my sensibility bound in layers of bandages and barely discernible. I found myself caught between the desires to gush out my grief — a need to be practical and make arrangements to meet Lisa's mum at the airport early the following morning — and an ardent attempt to affect normality for Andy. Evidently I was less than entirely successful in this latter regard for, in the midst of moulding a moat around his elaborate sandcastle, Andy stopped, stabbed his spade into a turret and asked, 'What's wrong, Dad?' He'd caught me unawares. I'd been thinking about Lisa, trying to remember our last conversation. 'Are you sad about Mum?'

'A bit,' I confessed. 'You?'

'I'll miss her,' he said. 'But I'm glad she's happy where she is. She wouldn't want us to be sad, would she?'

'No, she wouldn't,' I admitted, offering to buy him another ice-lolly as a means of changing the subject.

This curious case of role-reversal, whereby Andy consoled me rather than me consoling him, was repeated that night as I tucked him into bed. But while it touched me, his ready acceptance of his mother's death disconcerted me. He seemed to have swallowed whole my fairy tale about God and angels and heaven without question. I suppose that was to be expected. I had never lied to him before, so why should he suspect me of having lied to him then?

Alone that night, I reflected on the day. I sat out on the veranda to contemplate the stars and wallow in self-pity, postponing my appointment with an empty bed. When I did eventually retire for the night, my gradual shift into slumber was interrupted by that first involuntary jerk and, wide-awake, I got up to cuddle into Andy.

The following morning I was woken by a knock at the door. I jumped out of bed and yanked it open to discover the same policeman who'd stood there the morning before. Once again, he bowed, removed his helmet and offered me an item of jewellery. For a moment I didn't understand, and then I noticed his expression, imploring me to comprehend in order to spare him the ordeal of attempting an explanation, and I took the crucifix from his hand, dangled it before my eyes, and realised what it meant.

I searched the apartment, shouting Andy's name. There was no response. The policeman waited at the doorway, fidgeting with the rim of his helmet until I stopped and looked at him. He had something in his hand that he was offering me. It was a letter. I was afraid to read it. Instead, I searched the empty rooms one last time. It was then, and only then, that I discovered Andy's last, undelivered, letter to you (the letter it is my fervent hope to finally deliver to you in person on Andy's behalf in the very near future) being used as a bookmark in his copy of *The Adventures of Huckleberry Finn*, and pocketed it, furtively, to be pored over as soon as I was alone. Eventually, resigned to Andy's absence, I approached the policeman, terrified that the letter he held would confirm my worst fear.

'We found this with the crucifix,' he said, handing me the letter.

This is what I read:

Dear Dad,

I've gone to be with Mum. I was missing her too much. I'll miss you too, but I know you'll come and see us soon. Hope you won't miss us too much. We'll be having fun in heaven playing with God and his angels. Bye!

Love, Andy xxx

chapter nine

an envelope without an address

'WHY DO YOU SIT THERE, looking like an envelope without an address?'

Yanked from the familiar comfort of my morbid ruminations to find myself sitting hunched up on a bench beneath the flag-pole in Queen's Park, I turned, startled, to assess the stranger who had materialised beside me, invading my body space despite the availability of an identical empty bench nearby. He was a sallow-skinned, callow youth with black-rimmed sunken eyes weary and worn by a burden seemingly too great for his tender years to bear.

'Sorry?' I stalled.

'Mark Twain,' he said. 'I never knew what he meant, until I saw you just now.'

I didn't know how to respond to this, so I didn't.

'Nice sunrise,' he commented. I looked to see it seep up the sky from the horizon like watercolour paint and nodded.

'Mark Twain,' he said. I turned to see him extend a hand for me to shake. I shook it and mumbled my own name.

'I'm a namesake,' he added.

Then, at the conclusion of a protracted hesitation, during which I received the distinct impression that he was weighing up what my reaction might be if he were to take a leap of faith and make me a proposal which lay beyond the parameters of what might be considered appropriate pleasantries between two strangers, he bade me farewell, hesitated, once more, though thankfully not for as long as before, and, when I echoed his farewell, departed.

I was left pondering his hesitation. I waited till he'd disappeared over the brow of the hill and then set off in the opposite direction, speculating about his identity. When I passed through the park gates, for the first time in a long time I remembered Lisa's last words to me. They'd struck me as odd at the time, as if she'd been reciting a quotation — and it was only now that I felt certain that she had been, and whom it belonged to.

'There is in life only one moment and in eternity only one,' she'd said, in response to what, I no longer recall.

I may well have remembered what she'd said, but I remained mystified by what she'd meant by it. What intrigued me, though, was the thought that there might be a connection between Lisa's Mark Twain quotation and my encounter with his namesake. I wondered whether his hesitation could be explained by the fact that he'd been on the verge of divulging something about Lisa. Or was that fanciful speculation? After all, it implied that our meeting had been arranged by him, and it was not often that I was to be found sitting on a bench beneath the flagpole at Queen's Park at the break of dawn ... so how could he have arranged to meet me there — unless he'd been spying on me? Could he have been behind the sense I had of being watched the previous day? I considered this possibility before deciding that it was more likely that our encounter was a simple case of coincidence. After all, Mark Twain quotations are not exactly obscure. I knew a few myself: 'Truth is good manners; manners are a fiction,' for example.

Still, the more I thought about our conversation, the odder it seemed and I considered returning to search for the namesake to confirm that our encounter could be put down to chance rather than design, but realised that he could be anywhere by now, so, instead, I proceeded on my way home, my thoughts already returning to the familiar haunting ground from which they'd been so rudely interrupted by the namesake's untimely intrusion.

chapter ten

suicide note

THE IRREPRESSIBLE OPTIMISM of the 'Bye!' in Andy's suicide note nailed me to the crucifix of my lie; the lie to myself as much as my lie to him.

I sought some evil past deed I'd committed to explain why I'd been singled out for such divine retribution, a search which contradicted the conviction of my atheism, but conviction had long since been replaced by a maggoty mass of contradiction.

As I continually replay the reshot version of my internal scene of our last morning, my monologue has undergone a radical revision so that, when Andy wakes and asks me where his mum is, instead of seducing him with beautiful lies spawned from a cowardly attempt at shielding him from the terrible truth, I grasp the thistle and tell him the truth, relate the facts as I know them to be and answer his questions with unflinching honesty. Of course, revision is easy in the safety cushion of retrospective introspection where, with the benefit of hindsight, I know that, instead of shielding Andy from the truth, my lies had been accepted as truth, with the result that, rather than recoil from the truth, he'd embraced the lie. With the benefit of hindsight I suspect that I'd underestimated his inherent resilience and capacity for coping with bereavement. I truly believe that the terrible truth would not have proved fatal, as the seductive lie had shown itself to be.

Beneath my own grief lay a stratum of mortification at the improbability of losing my partner and my son within twenty-four hours. As a plot twist in a work of fiction it would have been rejected outright as implausible melodrama but, unfortunately for me, reality had no truck with such literary considerations, concerning itself solely with fate; and fate, whether literary critics liked it or not, had an insatiable appetite for sensation and tragedy; an appetite which my paper stood as daily testament.

'Bye!' Andy had written.

'Your son's handwriting — yes?' asked the policeman, indicating the letter. I nodded. 'He could swim?' he asked, mimicking the breaststroke.

'Yes,' I confirmed, 'but he was only seven.'

The policeman nodded and fidgeted with his helmet, a habit I recognised. He asked me to accompany him. I thought he was leading me back to the morgue but, instead, he took me to the police station where, in a cramped, windowless room, a uniformless and perfect English-speaking colleague joined him to probe me thoroughly, though not without sensitivity, about the last known movements of Lisa and Andy, recording my replies with a paper and pen and a tape machine, occasionally prompting me to speak louder 'for the benefit of the tape', a phrase whose familiarity, through overhearing its frequent recurrence in a popular thrice-weekly ITV police series which Lisa watched religiously, made me feel as though I was acting out a part in one of its episodes, just as I'd felt I'd been acting out a scene when I'd visited the mortuary no more than twenty-four hours earlier.

I don't know whether he was a literary critic in his spare time, but evidently the uniformless policeman shared that profession's disdain for credibility-straining coincidence.

At the conclusion of this protracted question and answer session I was told that the note, complete with child-sized fingerprints, and the crucifix had been hung on a nail on a post at the end of the pier. I learned that Andy's body had not yet been found but that, given the letter, they would continue to search the sea for him.

chapter eleven

forgery

ON MY RETURN HOME, there was a letter addressed to Andy amongst the scattered pile of junk mail and bills littering the hall. It wasn't till I saw his name on the envelope that I finally gave up hope of him ever being found alive. I held the envelope up to examine its postmark and realised that Andy would never read the letter inside it. For a few moments I mulled over the morality of reading it myself then succumbed to temptation and tore it open. It was from you.

It was written with a red felt tip pen in an intimate style brimming with zest. Its summery air of undiluted idealism and implicit faith in the omnipresence of good, devoid of any inkling of evil, made me despair of my own long-lost innocence. You wrote of a family holiday travelling through the Rockies in a burnt-orange Volkswagen camper van with your mum and dad and your little brother. You gave a detailed account of an action-packed fortnight, written in an unaffected style that conveyed the adventure of your holiday. Your anecdotes at the expense of your parents made me laugh aloud. Your protectiveness towards your brother, though never explicitly stated, shone through each line and made me cry — pathetic, perhaps, and damning evidence of a cloying sentimentality, maybe, but a welcome, albeit belated, release, for it shames me to confess that I'd been unable to produce so much as a single tear throughout the unfolding double-tragedy of Lisa and Andy.

I wondered what response to the letter, if any, would be considered appropriate. I cowered from the obligation of informing you about Andy's tragedy. Your innocence seemed far too precious for me to slaughter with the truth. Seeking a way to avoid having to tell you about Andy, an ingenious solution occurred to me: I would write to you, but I would assume Andy's identity.

Morbidly excited by this devious scheme of deception (born from cowardice rather than altruism, however much I sought to convince myself that the reverse was true) I rushed to where Andy hid his stockpile of your correspondence and passed many, too many, hours poring over it to trace the trajectory of his relationship with you. I soon became absorbed with these letters. I found that they helped me cope with the trauma of my double-tragedy. The insight they gave me into Andy's thoughts, as perceived by way of your replies to them, accentuated my loss; an accentuation that I masochistically relished because my loss had come to define me and the more keenly I felt it, the more readily I could accept that part of me was still alive.

I became obsessed with the idea of being able to read the letters Andy had sent you. Aside from the solitary final artefact, I possessed only one side of the story and so could only fantasise about the other, where Andy's thoughts, written in his own fair hand, lay waiting to be discovered in a corresponding stockpile of letters, no doubt tucked out of sight in a corner of your bedroom thousands of miles away in Vancouver Island.

The absence of these letters gnawed at my insides a little more each day. I dreamed about the insights into Andy they contained until the importance I attached to them grew to the extent that I began to equate their return to the return of Andy himself; a metaphorical resurrection maybe, but the only reason I could think of to postpone my appointment with Andy and Lisa.

The lack of any letters from Lisa, and the lack of any prospect of finding any letters from Lisa, made her death final to me. She was dead and gone and, though it grieved me so, her absence was irrevocable. But the fact that Andy had never been found, and the thought that one day I might be able to read his correspondence, kept him alive in my imagination. His words had outlived him. They still existed, somewhere; and maybe, somewhere, so did he.

It was some time before I dared attempt to compose a reply to you. When I finally did, I tried to imagine I was Andy's age. As well as the one, vital letter of Andy's to you I had in my possession, I was helped in this regard by reference to the bundles of letters my own pen-pal, Liam, had written to me and so it was that I set sail on a voyage of rediscovery of my own long-forgotten youth.

I was struck by the innocence and naivety I encountered there and wondered whether the tone employed by Andy would be similar to that employed by Liam, a notion that only made my hunger to read for myself his correspondence to you more acute. Once innocence had been lost, could it be rediscovered? Could the lessons of experience be unlearned? What a fabulous notion, for, if there was one thing that rereading the letters Liam had written to me as a seven-year-old had shown me, it was that, rather than leading me towards happiness, the knowledge that came with experience had led me astray.

If the recapture of innocence was to be possible, I suspected that the process would at least be as laborious as that entailed in the gaining of experience. In order to short circuit that protracted process, I resigned myself to the challenge of faking innocence for the purpose of assuming Andy's identity for writing to you. I emptied Andy's shelves of school jotters and concentrated on copying his handwriting and prose style.

Finally, after many monotonous evenings devoted to hours of rigorous practice, the day arrived when I felt I was ready to attempt a passable imitation and, after countless botched drafts, a few days later I posted a brief reply to you, which, though it had taken an immense time and effort to compose, contrived to appear spontaneous.

The ensuing weeks dragged by and were endured agonising over whether you would accept my forgery as an original or see through my attempted fraud. A fortnight after I posted the letter, I adopted the habit of waiting for the postman to deliver the post before departing for work, my dread and anticipation compounding each successive morning until, finally, one rain-soaked Wednesday, a reply arrived and, with trembling hands, I tore open the damp envelope to find, with a disproportionate sense of relief, that you had fallen for my fraud.

My next letter only took half as long to compose as the first and the one after that half as long again until my confidence had scaled such heights that the spontaneity of the letters, at least, was genuine. And, though it had never been my intention to prolong this deception, I soon became addicted to the regular receipt of your correspondence. I revelled in my adopted identity, which afforded me the opportunity to imagine what kind of life Andy might have lived whilst giving me a second chance to live my own. The correspondence let me escape from my double-tragedy into an irresistible world of rosy optimism. And the longer it continued, the harder it became to bring it to a conclusion. Each time I promised myself that I would sign off, a letter would arrive from you of such innocent intimacy that I realised that the cruelty or brevity necessary to kill it off lay beyond me.

After a long time I felt able to return to work on *Original Harm*, which I'd neglected, though virtually all my previous motivations for writing it had been rendered redundant. I decided to proceed with it primarily for Andy, to atone him, and for myself, to postpone my celestial reunion with Andy and Lisa. The routine of editing the paper's letters page during the day, writing *Original Harm* in the evening and corresponding with you preoccupied me and kept me alive. *Original Harm* was an extended love letter to my partner and son, its joint dedicatees. Perhaps that partly explained why I was so sensitive to criticism of it and leapt to its defence when I found it to be the subject of a savage attack by Niamh Toe in the pages of my own paper. I wasn't defending myself. I was defending the cherished memory of my beloveds, which I felt had been desecrated.

Remembering that review reminded me of the blackmailer's letter. I popped into a twenty-four-hour garage to pick up a copy of the paper to see if the story had made the front page. It had. The story was illustrated with a photograph of the actual letter. Examining it anew, I was once again struck by the notion that there was something familiar about the handwriting.

PART THREE

thai omen

chapter twelve

the front page (1)

AT THE FOOT OF A FRONT PAGE dominated by an in-depth eye-witness account of a running riot in George Square — caused by the unforeseen invasion by a militant mob of peace protesters of a peaceful protest by pro-war campaigners calling for the government to send ground troops into central Europe as part of a UN peacekeeping force; a clash which resulted in a fatal stabbing (of a twenty-one-year-old, five months pregnant district council receptionist unfortunate enough to have been passing through the square on her lunch break when the riot had erupted around her) and eleven people admitted to hospital with a variety of injuries ranging from concussion to broken limbs to surface cuts and contusions — the following unattributed story appeared:

KIDNAP DEATH THREAT

We have received an anonymous letter from a kidnapper threatening to kill a hostage if we do not publish it in full on the front page of today's paper.

The hostage is named in the letter (shown opposite) as Mr Ian Thome, who recently wrote to us in defence of a novel against a critical review, which itself appeared earlier in the week.

The kidnapper warns that 'intolerance will not be tolerated' and that he will slit Mr Thome's throat unless we print his letter and promise 'never again to publish such a misguided defence of pernicious propaganda'.

Mr Thorne's letter had been written in response to a review of *Original Harm*, a first novel by Tom Haine. The reviewer, Niamh Toe, criticised it for what she regarded as the wrong-footed stance it took on its central theme of abortion.

Mystery surrounds the identity of the kidnapper. The letter is not thought to have originated from any of the known extremist pro-life organisations and none has accepted responsibility for it. Rather, it is thought that the kidnapper is most likely to be a lone fanatic bearing a personal grudge against Mr Thorne.

The letter proceeds to direct a death threat at our editor if he should fail to comply with its demands and includes a reference to Mr Craig Liddell, a book reviewer, found murdered in a city centre hotel room earlier this year.

Mr Liddell's murder remains unsolved and it would appear that the anonymous kidnapper of Mr Thorne is claiming responsibility for it.

John Kerr, editor, has condemned the death threat as 'a sickening and cowardly attack on free speech'.

See feature page 7 and leader page 11

I was made breathless from the effects of a potent cocktail of excitement at the notoriety with which *Original Harm* had become associated and fear for the inevitability of my imminent discovery. If Chris the Crossword Compiler had spotted the anagrammatic link, then it wouldn't take long for some of the paper's more astute readers to deduce it too and proceed to speculate about the motivation lurking behind it until they uncovered me, at which point they might be excused for leaping to the conclusion that there was a direct link between the identity of the individual behind the anagrammatic link and the identity of the kidnapper.

It occurred to me that another motivation for seeking the swift identification of the kidnapper, in addition to securing the safe release of the innocent hostage whose ordeal I had inadvertently orchestrated, was to deflect any such suspicion from falling on me.

I hurried home to spread out the paper on my kitchen table and pore over the feature and the leader column, foraging for any new and potentially valuable snippets of information to help me plan an appropriate course of action.

The feature on page seven gave the background behind the front-page teaser by detailing accounts of Niamh Toe's review of *Original Harm* and Ian Thome's letter defending the book. In an inset item, Kirsty Baird re-reviewed *Original Harm* (broadly echoing, though in less strident terms, Niamh Toe's critique — given that she'd commissioned it and already edited it, she could hardly contradict it) whilst, in a neighbouring piece, Professor Paul Buchanan of the University of Glasgow, a specialist on the psychology of terrorism (I had published several of his letters on previous occasions) speculated about the motives of the black-mailer and whether or not the death threat should be taken seriously (he felt that, on balance, it would be 'folly to dismiss it out of hand').

As I finished the article and turned to page eleven, the rustle of the paper told me that my hands were trembling. When I saw the leader column, my anticipation was engulfed by exasperation as I read a Mark Twain quotation. I'll reproduce the column for you verbatim, as always.

'It is by the goodness of God that in our country we have those three unspeakably precious things: freedom of speech, freedom of conscience, and the prudence never to practice either of them.'

Perhaps Mark Twain is right and this paper has indeed been imprudent in practising what it preaches but, if so, we make no apologies for that.

Papers like this one exist to report news — not become entangled in it; but when we do, it is imperative that we defend the twin freedoms of speech and conscience, the very poles of the axis around which we revolve.

Yesterday we were presented with a letter which left us confronting something of a dilemma: whilst it represented a direct attack on the aforementioned principles upon which we were founded, if we were to leap instantly to defend these principles, then an individual would be murdered as a direct consequence.

Letters from outraged cranks making empty threats are not unknown to newspapers and, usually, they are disposed of without further ado, or else the offending items are turned over to the police.

However, we decided to make an exception of yesterday's letter.

We did so because we felt there was sufficient reason to believe that the threat it contained was not empty, but loaded. That, certainly, was the conclusion arrived at by Professor Paul Buchanan, an expert on such matters whose advice we solicited.

The chief factor in our decision to take the threat seriously was the link made between the murder of the book reviewer Craig Liddell, which the kidnapper appears to claim responsibility for, and the threat to the life of Ian Thome: both were advocates of free speech and it would appear to be more than mere coincidence that Craig Liddell's throat was cut and that this is the same method of execution with which Ian Thome is threatened.

The burden of this specific and direct threat of a fatal consequence proved too great for us to ignore and meant that, in this unique instance, and after prolonged agonising over the dilemma with which it presented us, we opted to publish the kidnapper's letter.

We did so because we recognised that, ultimately, our precious freedoms of speech and conscience are incorporeal and, whilst priceless to us, when weighed against a human life, worthless.

No principle should be considered absolute: if it is accepted as such, we soon forget the reasoning behind it and our defence of it descends swiftly into a mire of blind faith. Instead it must be subjected constantly to rigorous revaluation and revision and tested against each particular circumstance that presents itself.

In this particular circumstance we felt that the most appropriate way to demonstrate our faith in free speech was by publishing the kidnapper's letter seeking to deny that very right — not because we were bowing to the kidnapper's demands, but because, through the act of publishing his abhorrent message, we reinforce the right of free speech.

There is, undoubtedly, an irony in demonstrating the right of free speech by publishing a letter attacking that very right, but life is awash with ironies, and this is not the only irony in this matter.

A further irony is that the kidnapper's death threat has given *Original Harm*, the book it is so desperate to suppress, prime exposure, without which it would more than likely have languished in obscurity.

The kidnapper's reprehensible methods, too, will alienate all public sympathy for his arguments and, instead, direct it towards the novel he so despises.

It is worth stressing that, by publishing the kidnapper's letter, we have not abandoned, but reinforced, our principles. We abhor the actions of the kidnapper and this paper will be fighting for freedom of speech and conscience long after he is dead and gone because we consider such freedoms as fundamental to this country.

It is also worth noting that, whilst we have opted to publish the letter on the front page of today's newspaper, we refuse to comply with the kidnapper's demand that we undertake not to publish such views as those expressed by Ian Thome again — whatever threats, or subsequent actions, the kidnapper might make.

Craig Liddell was an advocate of free speech and he was murdered. Ian Thome is an advocate of free speech and he is threatened with murder. This paper advocates free speech but refuses to pass a death sentence on Ian Thome.

One final irony: whilst we are unwilling to sacrifice a single human life on the altar of free speech, we simultaneously believe that this principle is ultimately of infinitely greater importance than any individual.

I struggled to comprehend the implication of the inclusion of a Mark Twain quotation in the leader column; it really did seem a case of a coincidence too far, but if its presence could not be explained by coincidence, then why was it there? I had no answer, which unsettled me, and so I proceeded to reread the front page and the feature and the leader column with mounting irritation. Finally admitting defeat to the Twain enigma, I cast the paper aside and gulped down cornflakes, showered, shaved, shit, caught the 44 into work and scanned the paper once more en route.

chapter thirteen

the price of free speech

As I REREAD THE LEADER COLUMN on the bus into work I could see that its author was attempting to persuade himself, as much as his readers, of his arguments; seeking to salve his conscience and justify the paper's capitulation to the kidnapper's demands. The column amounted to little more than a pre-emptive defence against anticipated criticisms.

Then it struck me that I had no idea who the leader writer of the paper was. It had never occurred to me before. It was not a column that I was in the habit of reading, despite the fact that it appeared alongside the letters. Perhaps, given the inclusion of the Mark Twain quotation, the leader writer was implicated in the affair?

Flicking back through the paper to reread the article on page seven to see if I'd missed any other Twain quotations, my eye was caught by a black and white photograph that dominated page nine. It showed a mass of scattered bodies of slaughtered men, women and children in a village square — twenty or thirty corpses left to rot where they'd been hacked or bludgeoned or shot; flies swarming over the skewed limbs and mud and blood drenched rags — a grotesque image which, for the first time, despite having read numerous reports of the atrocities, forced me to realise the horror of the genocide. It was one thing to read the gruesome statistics of ethnic cleansing and conceive the horror; it was quite another to confront the photographic evidence.

On arrival at the office, I squeezed into the crowded lift to the first floor and, unable to resist the temptation, before I even removed my coat and hat, stopped and glanced at the purple paperweight pinning down the pile of letters on my desk.

'Morning,' sighed Kirsty Baird, teacup in hand, on her way to the kitchen.

'Morning,' I obliged.

'How's the missus?' she asked.

'Fine,' I smiled. 'She's fine.'

I removed my raincoat and jacket, took off my homburg, hung up my umbrella and ventured into the kitchen to make myself a cup of peppermint tea. But before I started slitting the envelopes, I put on my specs, after wiping the lenses with a crumpled hankie to which I'd applied a sliver of saliva, booted up the computer to start printing out the e-mails, shuffled and stapled the faxes and rifled through the envelopes in the hope of discovering an exotic postmark. By this time, my tea had cooled sufficiently to allow me my first slurp.

A small padded envelope attracted my attention but, noticing that I'd been left voicemail, I was distracted momentarily from opening it. I keyed my code into the phone and listened to a Stephen Hawking-esque monotone intone 'Intolerance will not be tolerated' and felt the full weight of responsibility for the commitment of a personal atrocity on an unsuspecting innocent.

I opened the Jiffy bag and extracted a blue velvet jewellery box that I prized open with all the tentativeness of a trainee bomb disposer. Inside, on a cushion of white satin, nestled a transparent convex disc similar in size and shape to a contact lens. Puzzled, I re-examined the envelope and fished out an overlooked postcard with 'The price of free speech' scrawled in familiar bog-standard handwriting on one side and 'Sometimes life imitates art' on the other.

My phone rang and Kerr summoned me into his smoke-filled aquarium.

'This is Ms Pardos,' he said, indicating a figure lurking in a corner, shrouded in his smoke.

She was dressed in black and when she approached me, measuredly, the grey clouds that had enveloped her swirled into the space she vacated and trailed after her, beseeching her to stay in their embrace. Her footsteps made no sound. The way she moved conveyed that she was, and always would be, at ease with herself and with any given situation that might present itself to her to do with as she pleased. She moved as if she was weighing me up and deciding when to pounce.

'Pleased to meet you,' I said. She was only looking at me but it felt as if she was inspecting me.

'We've met before,' she said. It was only then that I recognised her as the girl with the flawless Cadbury-coloured skin, bee-stung lips and swaying hips I'd mistaken for Niamh Toe at the library the previous day.

'Ms Pardos is investigating yesterday's death threat,' said Kerr.

'Are you a detective?' I asked.

'*Private* detective,' she clarified.

'Then you'd better take a look at this,' I said, handing her the jewellery box.

I took her to the Space Bar, where she ordered coffees and settled down to quiz me.

'So it wasn't just coincidence that you were in the library yesterday?' I asked.

'Coincidences are rare,' she said, stirring half a teaspoonful of brown sugar into her coffee; hypnotising me with the circular motion of her sugar pink nails.

'Have you been following me?'

'Something like that.'

I was unsure how to respond, so I didn't.

'Are you scared?' she asked.

'Should I be?'

'Perhaps.'

We sipped our coffees.

'Tell me about yourself,' she said.

'What d'you want to know?'

'You decide.'

'I'm the letters page editor,' I said. 'I edit the letters page.'

'Is that it?' she said.

'What d'you want to know?'

'How long have you been the letters page editor?'

'Too long.'

'You don't like it?'

'No. I was being facetious. It's a trait. I love it. I've done it for ten years.'

'You're in a rut?'

'I've got to get out of it.'

'You're right — it is a trait,' she said. 'Are you married?'

'No.'

'Kids?'

I shook my head. 'Is this an interrogation?'

'Does it feel like an interrogation?'

'Yes.'

'Why don't *you* ask *me* some questions?'

'I'd need to be interested in the answers.'

'Aren't you?' she said, adopting a wounded tone.

I shrugged. 'Are *you* married?' I asked.

'No.'

'Kids?'

'No.'

'Available?'

She didn't answer.

'Sorry, I can't help myself. Why were you in the library at the same time as me?'

'I'd had a phone call instructing me to be there.'

'Who from?'

'It was anonymous.'

'So was the letter. D'you think the phone call was from the kidnapper?'

'Maybe.'

'Was the voice male or female?'

'I couldn't say for certain — it had been electronically tampered.'

'So, what's your next move?'

'We'll analyse the contents of your jewellery box.'

We sipped our coffees.

'Yesterday you mistook me for Niamh Toe,' she said. 'Did you find her?'

'I thought I did but now I'm not sure.'

'Why were you looking for her?'

'I wanted to speak to her about the letter.'

'Why?'

'I thought she might have written it.'

'Why?'

'Because Thome's letter was critical of her review.'

'And you thought she might have kidnapped him for revenge?'

I shrugged.

'It doesn't sound very likely, does it?' she suggested.

'No,' I admitted.

'Who do you think wrote the letter?'

'I've no idea. Who do you think made the anonymous phone call?'

'Why didn't you take the letter immediately to your editor?'

'I wanted to establish if it was genuine before pestering him with a crank.'

'Did you?'

'Not totally — but I don't think it's from a crank.'

'Why not?'

'Something about the way it's written — and the fact that I received that this morning,' I said, indicating the jewellery box.

We sipped our coffees.

'Have you read *Original Harm*?' she asked.

'No.'

'Do you know anything about its author, Tom Haine?'

'No.'

'He doesn't exist,' she said.

'Excuse me?'

'It's a pseudonym.'

'How do you know that?'

'I asked the publisher.'

'Who's the publisher?'

'Tina something — Home,' she said.

'And how did you get in touch with her?'

'Through the PO Box number on the title page.'

'So who *did* write the book?' I asked, attempting not to sound perturbed.

'I don't know yet. I didn't press the issue, but I will. Have you heard of Toni Mahe?' she asked, pronouncing it *May*. I'd always pronounced it *Ma-hay*.

'No. Should I know him?'

'Not necessarily. Count yourself lucky. What do you make of The Amino?'

'They're just fictional, aren't they?'

'That's right,' she said. 'They're in that book you haven't read.'

We sipped our coffees.

'What are you prepared to do to get out of it?'

'Out of what?'

'The rut.'

'What rut?'

'The rut of being a letters page editor. You said you'd been in the job too long.'

'I also said I loved it,' I said. 'If you're going to convict me of facetiousness then you better handcuff me now — I confess — guilty as charged.'

We sipped our coffees.

'Is there anything else you want to tell me?' she asked.

'Like what?'

'Nothing,' she said, her patience run out. 'Call me if anything occurs to you.'

She rose from her chair, then seemed to change her mind and sat back down.

'What do you believe in?' she asked in a fresh tone.

'What d'you mean?'

'Nothing,' she said.

She left me mulling over our conversation, struggling to resist an urge to lick her lipstick trace off her cup and run after her to confess my disastrous deception.

'I believe in you,' I said to myself.

chapter fourteen

expulsion from in a robot

ON THE WAY BACK TO THE OFFICE I reflected on the café conversation. I suspected that Pardos knew all about my pseudonyms. I was troubled by the thought of her visiting *Original
Harm*'s publisher because I'd published it myself. So who was
Tina Home? I'd immediately recognised the name as yet another
'I am not he' anagrammatically-derived pseudonym and was
anxious to learn the true identity of who was masquerading as
my publisher. Or might Tina Home have been a concoction by
Pardos designed to prompt me to contradict Home's existence
and unwittingly divulge the extent of my implication in the affair?

The vast majority of letters that morning were concerned with
the escalation of war in central Europe, as I knew they would
be. Whilst the majority of them were in support of the government's policy of direct intervention, a significant minority took
an opposing view. I had only partly digested the events leading
up to the war and felt unqualified to take a particular stance on
the issue. That morning, I read a couple of articles that I hoped
would clarify it for me — a pro-interventionist piece by our chief
political editor and an anti-interventionist column by our foreign
editor alongside it — but, instead, they succeeded only in mud-
dling me further. I read the first article and was convinced by its

logic, then read the second and was convinced by its logic too. I could see both sides of the argument, but couldn't see where I stood in relation to it.

A couple of hours later Pardos called to inform me, in her usual deadpan delivery, that, according to her forensic laboratory contact, the jewellery box had not contained a contact lens, but a lens extracted from a human eye, pausing momentarily to allow the full horror of this discovery to register before proceeding to ask me once more if I could tell her anything. Fighting to suppress a gag reflex, through eyes squeezed tight in a forlorn attempt to shield myself from being forced to contemplate the excruciating pain of having an eyeball sliced open should, God forbid, the torture victim happen to have been alive at the time, again, I answered that I could not.

Having been instructed by Kerr that morning to inform him immediately of any news concerning the jewellery box, I relayed Pardos's information to him then went to the kitchen to refresh myself with a cup of peppermint tea. The kitchen was occupied by Dick and Hill, our sister evening paper's investigative reporters who shared by-lines and just about everything else besides (from, it had been rumoured, wives, to the chicken tikka masala they were currently devouring with such gusto), huddled together, comparing notes in conspiratorial tones about their latest investigation.

Dick and Hill were a pair of old-style tabloid hacks that, over the years, had acquired the seen-it-all-before demeanour common to their profession. Nothing much could impress or surprise them. Their grasp of grammar might have been rudimentary, their prose might have required polish, but they were recognised by their peers as the best investigative journalists in the country by far. Their contacts throughout the city's black market were comprehensive and the envy of their competitors. Between them they knew all the local loan sharks, dealers, bookies, pimps, DSS-scam landlords and underworld-connected licensees and, because Dick was Protestant and Hill Catholic, they were able to cover both sides of the city's notorious sectarian divide. It was said that the police were constantly contacting them for help with their enquiries but that they adhered to a strict professional code of guaranteed anonymity for their sources.

There were better writers than Dick and Hill on the newspaper, but there were no better journalists. Their ability to deliver a regular supply of scoops, a consequence of their deft skill in extracting information from interviewees intent on maintaining a dignified silence, was renowned. It was an ability that could partly be explained by the fact that they spoke the same language as their interviewees. They had grown up in the same streets as their interviewees. They shared a common cultural history. Both interviewers and interviewees were ingrained with a breadth and depth of knowledge of Glasgow unique to the lifelong native and this mutual bond led to guards being dropped and confidences being exchanged. Dick and Hill were always working. Whether they were at the football (they shared an encyclopaedic knowledge about Scottish football and were hero-worshipped by, and role models for, the sports desk pups) or the pub (they seemed to exist on a never-ending diet of fags and shorts), they were invariably immersed in in-depth discussions about their latest story or snooping around people they knew that knew people who could help them progress a lead. Their lives were their work. Their work was their lives. There was something noble about that and I admired them for it.

I was about to leave the kitchen when I realised they were talking about The Amino. I paused in the doorway just long enough to overhear Dick mention Holyrood Quadrant, an address that struck me as familiar. Back at my desk, I extracted a crumpled piece of paper from my breast pocket and confirmed it to be the same address — the address I'd found in the phone book the day before — Ian Thome's address.

I decided to pay it a return visit.

Once more, I pounded on the bottle-green storm doors, but still there was no reply. I had just resigned myself to the fact of another vain attempt to find the unfortunate Ian Thome when I heard a bolt being unlocked. A tall, pasty-faced apparition wrapped in a floral duvet slouched shivering in the doorway, scratching his scalp, a half-eaten tin of alphabetti spaghetti in his hand, waiting for me to explain my presence.

'Sorry to disturb you,' I apologised, 'I'm looking for Ian Thome.'

'You've found him,' he yawned.

'Oh,' I said. He'd thrown me completely.

'You thought I'd been kidnapped, didn't you?' he said.

'I did,' I admitted.

'I've had reporters at my door all morning,' he said.

'Sorry to disturb you,' I repeated, taking my leave.

I was left pondering the possibility that I might not have been responsible for the torture of an innocent after all. Perhaps it was all an elaborate hoax perpetrated by someone who had somehow deduced that I was both the author of *Original Harm* and the letter-writer defending it against criticism? But who would do that and why? The only person who I knew had deduced the anagram linking my pseudonyms was Chris the Crossword Compiler, but though he'd realised the link between them, there was no evidence yet that he'd linked them to me. I couldn't conceive of Chris scheming anything so sinister yet, nevertheless, I made a point of revisiting him, just to reassure myself.

As I'd anticipated, Chris soon dispelled any doubts I'd entertained about his innocence, but then, whilst rummaging amidst precarious mountains of well-thumbed puzzle books, thesauri, dictionaries and encyclopaedias, he mentioned a call he'd received less than an hour earlier which he thought might interest me.

The caller had phoned to complain about a clue Chris had used in the crossword of the day before: nine across, one word, eight letters — the clue, *expulsion from in a robot* — the solution, *abortion*. The caller had enquired whether he (Chris) considered it appropriate to insert such a morally offensive topic as the brutal murder of an innocent life into a family crossword puzzle which he (the caller) and his young son had enjoyed striving to complete for some time now.

'What did you say?' I enquired, starting to wonder why he was telling me this, worrying whether he *did* perhaps know that I'd written *Original Harm*, or whether he was raising the subject simply because of its relevance to that morning's front page.

'What *could* I say?' he said. 'If he'd been ranting or raving, it'd have been easier to defend myself and dismiss him as a lunatic —'

' — And if he hadn't flattered you by claiming to be a regular player of your crosswords,' I observed.

'He claimed to be calling, not just on behalf of himself, but in his capacity as spokesman for an organisation — '

'An organisation?'

'Yes —'

'What organisation?' I could hear the irritation rising in my voice but I couldn't help myself. My anxiety was inflating and I was impatient to have it deflated or validated before it burst.

'He claimed to be the spokesman for the Scottish chapter of something called The Amino,' said Chris. 'It was his name which I thought might interest you.'

'Oh?' I said, striving to feign nonchalance.

'Yeah — Noah Time.'

Chris waited to see that I had registered that this was yet another variation of an anagrammatically-derived 'I am not he' pseudonym.

'So what happened?' I enquired, struggling to contain my alarm.

'I sought to placate him as much as I could,' said Chris. 'I apologised and told him that no offence was intended. He insisted on registering an official complaint on behalf of his organisation, in writing, so, in an attempt to pre-empt that, and in order to have written evidence at my disposal should his complaint ever lead to awkward questions being asked requiring me to account for myself, I offered to put my apology in writing too — '

' — You have his address?'

'Here it is,' he said, handing it to me.

'Let's keep this between ourselves just now, OK?' I suggested.

I returned to my desk to find a pile of neglected mail waiting to be disembowelled. Searching in vain for my skean dhu letter opener, I eventually remembered that I'd slipped it into my raincoat pocket the day before (although amused at my own sense of drama, I put it back into my coat pocket before leaving the office that evening). Midway through the pile I was struck by the familiarity of the handwritten address on an envelope and knew before I opened it that it was from the kidnapper. This time I took care not to discard the envelope, which had no postmark (meaning that it must have been hand-delivered some time during the morning). Inside, on the same bog-standard paper and using the same bog-standard biro as before, appeared the following familiar scrawl.

Intolerance will not be tolerated.

Thank you for publishing my letter on the front page of today's paper; doing so saved Ian Thome from having his throat slit. I was, however, disappointed to note that you refused to promise never again to publish such a misguided defence of pernicious propaganda. Thome has duly suffered the consequences of your intransigence — I trust you received this morning's package.

I've decided to give you a second chance to make your promise. Failure to do so will result in Thome's death and your own capture and execution.

I marched straight into Kerr's smoky aquarium and plopped the letter down on his desk.

'What's this?' he demanded.

'A letter,' I said.

'I can see that. Who from?'

'The kidnapper.'

'What does he say?'

I relayed the contents of the letter to him. Only then did Kerr read it for himself.

'Fuck this,' he sighed, reaching for his phone.

He spoke briefly to Findlay then summoned his PA, instructing her to have ten copies of the letter in the boardroom in five minutes. Then he exited his aquarium and strode to the lift. We stepped out onto the top floor to find that the board had already convened. Kerr's PA slipped into the room and handed him copies of the letter. The board members took their seats around the oval table as the hidden door in the oak panelling opened and White Whiskers shuffled through it and slumped into the nearest chair. Findlay cleared his throat, thanked the board members for their presence and invited Kerr to summarise the situation. Kerr rose to distribute the copies of the letter around the table, starting with White Whiskers. As he did so, he said, 'Gentlemen, the letter you have before you was received by our letters page editor,' here he nodded to me, 'no more than five minutes ago.'

I was stabbed by a sense of déjà vu.

'As you can see, it's another murder threat by the kidnapper. I've called this meeting to determine collectively an appropriate response — '

' — What's this bit about *I trust you received this morning's package*?' interrupted Whiskers, brandishing his photocopy.

'A lens extracted from a human eye was delivered through the post this morning,' explained Kerr, prompting a collective Pavlovian gasp as the board members, to a man, with the notable exception of Whiskers, reacted as I myself had done to the horror of this news.

'Was it indeed,' mumbled Whiskers, betraying not a flicker of consternation, before returning his attention to Kerr and, with a withering look, signalling for him to proceed.

'Well, so far as I can see, we're faced with two options: either we bow to the kidnapper's demands, or we refuse to have our editorial policy dictated to us by a kidnapper; a course of action with a potentially fatal consequence for the hostage.'

'Which option do you propose?' enquired Whiskers. Kerr stalled and surveyed the room, searching for clues to help him gauge the mood of the board. They remained inscrutable.

'Our leader column this morning explicitly states our refusal to have our editorial agenda set by a kidnapper,' he said. 'Unless we're willing to undertake an embarrassing U-turn, we can only take the second option and refuse the kidnapper's demands.'

'Agreed,' said Whiskers. 'But should we risk sacrificing the victim to spare our blushes?'

Kerr shrugged his shoulders. Once more Whiskers scanned the boardroom but no answer was forthcoming.

'What do *you* think?' he asked, his gaze coming to rest on me. 'It was your course of action we've followed so far. How do *you* propose we proceed?'

It was only then that I realised I'd assumed full responsibility for entangling the paper in this predicament (a responsibility which, to be fair, I couldn't really complain about, given that I *was* implicated in the creation of the predicament to a degree beyond which any of the board could possibly have imagined) and that my continued employment rested on my ability to emerge with a solution to the dilemma at hand. It is to my shame that what I said next was not what I believed, but what I believed Whiskers wanted to hear. What I said next was not spoken after due consideration of the dilemma I found myself confronting, but with the immediate aim of keeping me in gainful employment.

'I propose that, once again, we run the kidnapper's letter on the front page — he condemns himself with each word he writes,' I said, with as much conviction as I could muster.

'I propose that, once again, we run a front-page story about the kidnapper's demands within which we condemn his actions outright and set forth the thinking behind our own response to his demands. I propose that we seek to galvanise public support for our course of action by pre-empting any potential voices of dissent by sourcing a range of supportive statements from such influential groups as: a cross-party selection of MSPs; the police; human rights campaigners; religious leaders and a straw poll of public opinion. I propose that we spell out to this anonymous kidnapper that we will never be dictated to, that we stand resolutely by our editorial column of today and that no threat will sway us from our commitment to free speech. I propose that, once more, we exploit the opportunities for exclusivity that this second letter gives us. I propose that we set a substantial financial reward for any reader who can give us any information leading to the arrest of the kidnapper, that we set up a free dedicated hotline to that end and that we guarantee caller anonymity. I propose that we seek to lure this cowardly kidnapper from behind his shield of anonymity by inviting him to participate in a full and frank open debate about the issues at hand; offering him the opportunity to express his views in the paper in return for the release of the hostage — if he is sincere about his beliefs, then let's challenge him to express them, goad him into our arena, mock and ridicule him and assume the moral high ground...' Here I paused for breath and, I confess, dramatic effect; then, realising that I'd nothing more to say, I shrugged and said, 'That's what I propose.'

Unsure how to respond to my impassioned speech, the board glanced towards White Whiskers for guidance. Kerr leaned towards me.

'You propose that we sacrifice the hostage,' he said, in a voice only I could hear.

White Whiskers cleared his throat then began to nod.

chapter fifteen

something more than words

BEFORE LEAVING THE OFFICE I checked the address Chris the Crossword Compiler had given me. I was anxious to discover the true identity of Noah Time. I phoned Pardos, but the sound of her voice on answering the phone made me realise how cowardly my seeking her assistance would strike her, so I thought better of it and replaced the receiver without identifying myself then phoned a taxi instead.

It was already dark when I was deposited outside the Holiday Inn. I walked through a bustling foyer to the lifts where, after a deep breath, ignoring my mounting claustrophobia, I joined a small crowd entranced by the row of digits lighting intermittently above the doors and fidgeted with the letter opener in my pocket. Eventually the lift doors opened and the crowd exiting hustled past the crowd entering. I was the second last to enter. The doors were already closing when the last passenger squeezed in beside me. I felt her body pressing into mine and recognised her fragrance.

'Level three, right?' said Pardos, already stretching to push the button without awaiting my confirmation. I felt myself being elevated.

'I take it this is more than just coincidence,' I said.

'I've told you what I think about coincidences,' she replied.

'I guess you just can't keep away from me, can you?' I said.

'I see your trait's still intact,' she answered.

The doors pinged open and we exited.

'So tell me, how did you know I was going to the third floor?'

'I didn't. It was a guess.'

'It was a good guess.'

'I'm a good guesser.'

I'm relaying word for word my conversations with Pardos in an attempt to convey to you the way she talked. If, ripped from reality and reproduced without any attempt at editing them, her words lose their flavour, then, take my word for it, put that down to my decision not to even attempt to convey the infinite nuances and allusive suggestions of our conversations in print. I wouldn't know how to begin to try to do that; how to describe the way she said things; the hinted possibilities and hidden significance of the things she didn't say; the way she looked at me when she spoke to me, twisting the meaning of her words, rolling them around on her tongue, savouring their taste then spitting them out, as if she was telling me with a look that she knew that I knew that there was more to what she was telling me than what she was telling me and that this something more was in the *way* she was telling me — something more than words. I don't know how to begin to attempt to describe that, so I'm writing it as she said it, without embellishment, without editing out the banalities and repetitions of everyday speech, because I want to stay true to her voice and I suspect that if I were tempted to attempt to perfect it, I'd only succeed in destroying it.

The other main reason I'm relaying word for word my conversations with Pardos is that writing them down like this allows me to relive them anew, in a way, resurrects them — resurrects *her* — for me.

'Well, if you're such a good guesser, tell me the number of the room I'm going to,' I said.

'309,' she replied, without hesitation.

'You *are* a good guesser,' I said. 'How did you know that?'

'That was the room where Craig Liddell's body was found,' she said. 'Why are you going there?'

I told her about Chris the Crossword Compiler's phone call from Noah Time.

'And you think this Noah Time's the kidnapper?' she prompted.

'I thought it was worth asking him,' I said.

By this time we were standing directly outside room 309. I hesitated, waiting for her to advise me that the wise thing to do would be to turn around and go home.

'What are you waiting for?' she asked.

'Don't you have a gun or something?' I whispered, for fear the occupant of 309 should overhear us.

'Have I stepped into the pages of a thriller?' she asked aloud then, mimicking me, she whispered, 'And why are you whispering?'

I sighed and knocked on the door. Nobody answered. I knocked again, louder. Again there was no answer. I pressed my ear to the door but heard nothing.

'What shall we do?' I whispered.

'Here, try this,' said Pardos, handing me the key. 'He checked out this afternoon — paid by cash.'

Room 309 looked as perfunctorily pristine and characterless as any other three-star hotel room. As it had already been cleaned, there were no telltale clues to be gleaned.

'D'you think Noah Time's his real name?' she asked.

'Don't you?'

'No.'

'Who d'you think he is then?'

'I don't know yet.'

'So why's he calling himself Noah Time?'

'I don't know that either — but I'll find out.'

'I'm sure you will, sooner or later.'

'Sooner.'

We retired to a nearby café called the 13th Note, where we were lured down to the basement by the sounds of Latin American-flavoured jazz. A plaintive sax transported me back to a veranda in Port de Soller. When I closed my eyes I was lounging with Lisa in a post-coital bliss, still naked, on the veranda of our villa toking a joint and sipping sangria, listening to Jobim, inhaling the fragrance from the rampant bougainvillaea amongst the cluster of cypress trees.

'You must have loved her very much,' observed Pardos, returning me to the present.

'Who?' I asked.

'Whoever put that look in your eyes,' she said. I didn't reply. 'Sometimes you can love someone too much,' she added.

Just then an angelic blonde, barefoot and dressed in white, appeared onstage and sang a song in Spanish over a bossa nova beat. It must have been called something like *La Vida es una Sentencia de la Muerte* because that was the refrain which ended each verse.

On our way back upstairs for a bite to eat the band broke into a bossa nova version of Richard Strauss's *Also sprach Zarathustra* and I noticed its name written around the circumference of the skin of the bass drum: The Amino.

Over dinner Pardos remarked that she'd finished reading *Original Harm* earlier that evening and that she'd been captivated by it.

'It was one of those books where you'd love to meet the author and you wish the lead character was real — like Holden Caulfield or Tom Sawyer,' she said. 'You should read it.'

It took me all my limited powers of restraint to refrain from proclaiming authorship. The only thing that stopped me was a suspicion that this was exactly the response she was hoping for. Instead, I tried to turn the tables and take her by surprise.

'I paid Ian Thome a visit this afternoon,' I declared, anticipating a shocked response to the news that he hadn't been kidnapped after all. As usual, her reaction wasn't what I had expected.

'So did I,' she said. 'Did you speak to his flatmate?

'No.'

'That's because he's gone missing,' she said. I was confused.

'You think he's the kidnapper?'

'The flatmate?'

'Yes.'

'No, I think he's the victim.'

'You'll have to explain that,' I said.

'Mistaken identity,' she said.

'You'll have to explain that,' I repeated.

'Well, it's only a hunch, but my theory is that the kidnapper bungled and, instead of kidnapping Ian Thome, kidnapped his flatmate — a guy called Guy Fall — instead. Furthermore, my guess is that the kidnapper doesn't know that he's bungled. I think he thinks that his hostage is Ian Thome.'

'Do you intend to enlighten him?'

'Not yet.'

'Your theory presupposes that the kidnapper had not previously known Ian Thome.'

'No it doesn't.'

'Doesn't it?'

'No. It presupposes that the kidnapper had not previously *met* Ian Thome,' she corrected. At the time I saw no benefit to be derived from quibbling over semantics and so did not pursue that particular line of enquiry.

'And why would someone want to kidnap Ian Thome if they hadn't even met him?' I wondered.

'Well, it was made pretty clear in the kidnapper's letter that it had something to do with the letter written in response to the book review of *Original Harm*, the letter written, purportedly, by Ian Thome.'

'What d'you mean "purportedly"?'

'Well, my theory, for what it's worth, is that the Ian Thome you and I visited this afternoon is not the writer of that letter.'

'No?'

'No. My guess is that he's a namesake.'

'And I thought coincidences were rare,' I said.

I don't think Pardos appreciated my sarcasm because she stopped talking for a while.

'Talking about namesakes, you mentioned Tom Sawyer earlier,' I said.

'And what does that have to do with namesakes?'

'Well, it just so happens that I had an interesting encounter with Mark Twain early this morning,' I said.

For the first time, I saw a flicker of surprise flash across her face.

'Tell me more,' she said, so I recounted the dawn encounter by the flagpole at Queen's Park. 'Would you recognise him if you saw him again?' she asked.

'Of course,' I confirmed, my mental image of him already blurring as I spoke.

'Why d'you think an author would employ a pseudonym?' she asked.

'Why d'you ask me?'

'I'm interested in your answer. My hunch is that Tom Haine is a pseudonym but I can't think why the author, whoever he is, wouldn't use his real name. If *I'd* written *Original Harm*, I'd want recognition for it.'

'Not if you were uncertain how it would be received.'

'You think the author was concerned about adverse criticism?'

'I think it's a possibility. After all, by all accounts the book deals with a contentious issue, so perhaps he — or she — anticipated just the kind of extreme reaction that transpired. Why do you think Tom Haine's a pseudonym?'

'Because coincidences are rare and it simply strains credulity to put the fact that Tom Haine and Ian Thome and Noah

Time and Niamh Toe are all anagrams of "I am not he" down to coincidence.'

'You missed out Toni Mahe and Tina Home,' I said.

'Someone's fucking with us,' she said.

'Who?'

'I don't know, but my guess is that once we start unmasking whoever's hiding behind these pseudonyms we'll be well on our way to finding our kidnapper.'

'What about The Amino?'

'What about them? That's a story.'

'But what if life can imitate art? What if the name and philosophy has been appropriated by a *real* group of moral vigilantes — could the kidnapper not belong to such a group?'

'This is the second time tonight I feel as if I've stepped into the pages of a thriller,' said Pardos. 'Get real.'

It was my turn to fall silent.

'What if Tom Haine and Ian Thome were one and the same person?' she asked, as if the thought had just occurred to her (which I didn't believe for a second).

'Why Tom Haine and Ian Thome, why not Tina Home and Niamh Toe?'

'Because if, as you suggest, Tom Haine was used as a pseudonym by the author as a safeguard against unwanted criticism, it might just be that he proceeded to adopt a second pseudonym, Ian Thome, to answer those criticisms.'

'But where do Niamh Toe and Tina Home fit in?'

'What if the author of *Original Harm* was not only Tom Haine and Ian Thome but also adopted the pseudonym Niamh Toe as well?'

'Why would he criticise his own book?'

'Publicity. Hundreds of novels must be published every year and they all need the oxygen of publicity to save them from being pulped.'

'You're right,' I said. 'And perhaps the author of *Original*

Harm is also the kidnapper because now he's front page news.'

'Perhaps,' said Pardos, 'or perhaps he paid someone to do his dirty work for him.'

'It's not so much a thriller as a mystery,' I said.

'Is there anything you want to tell me?' she enquired.

I shook my head.

chapter sixteen

never the twain shall meet

WE PARTED AWKWARDLY with much left unsaid.

'What's your next move?' she asked. I shrugged.

'What's yours?' I asked. She shrugged.

'Is there anything you want to tell me?' she asked again. I considered declaring my love for her but shook my head and hailed her a taxi instead. I'd intended to invite her home but, whilst something about her manner told me she might not have spurned such an invitation, I found myself unable to articulate it.

It was only later, as I was crossing the Clyde, that I realised I'd been remaining faithful to the memory of Lisa. As soon as this dawned on me, I was seized by an aversion to the notion of returning to my empty flat. Instead, I acted on an impulse to pay a return visit to the flagpole at Queen's Park. I was hoping to replay my encounter with Mark Twain. There were some questions I wanted to ask him.

As I wandered up the hill, I reflected on Pardos and our conversations, belatedly realising what I should have said to her and would say to her the next time we met. I felt sure we would meet the next day. I was depending on it.

As I resumed my position on the same bench I had sat on in the early hours of the morning, I recalled Pardos's approving comments about *Original Harm* and filed them away for posterity. As I sat there I began, for the first time, to imagine the possibility of being able to reflect on *Original Harm* from an emotional distance. The view I glimpsed through this novel perspective was that, during the period of its composition, I had become immersed in, and to some extent obsessed with, the murder at the heart of the subject matter. As you know, *Original Harm* had partly been inspired by a real incident that had struck me as absurd and challenged my assumption of a commonly held moral code. It was this sense of absurdity that had fuelled the narrative and propelled me to query whether my code was out of kilter with the common morality or even — something I'd never questioned before — whether such a morality existed.

Writing the book was in part a process of working out for myself why the murder had struck me as absurd and whether the application of reason could help me comprehend and come to terms with it. But the more I considered the matter, the more absurd it became. Instead of my comprehension becoming clearer and an explanation emerging from behind the foreground fuzz of absurdity, my standpoint in relation to the incident became scuffed with uncertainty. *Original Harm* was also, in part, an attempt to trace the trajectory of that sense of unease.

As I sat yawning on the park bench, my ruminations slipped into the no-man's-land distinguishing fact from fiction and I found myself wandering aimless and alone in a forest. It was already dark and cold when I realised I was lost. In a panic I sought to retrace my steps, but instead of emerging into a clearing, I seemed to be ploughing deeper and deeper into a dense jungle. I started at each fresh squawk or squeal or unidentified rustle of leaves, searching the clawing branches with mounting trepidation till I tripped over thick undergrowth and sprained my left ankle. Then I glimpsed the moon glint off a luminous marble some distance ahead. Transfixed, I watched it approach then split in two, bobbing hypnotically through the dark as if suspended from an invisible thread. At the instant the bobbing became more pronounced, I wrenched myself from my trance with the dread realisation that a black panther was attacking me. My sprained ankle did not impede my escape. I was already incapable of movement — of breathing even. Paralysed, I sprawled, rooted, defenceless and waiting to be mauled as the panther pounced: its jaws open; its fearsome fangs visible; its flesh-tearing claws raised...

I awoke with a start to find Mark Twain seated beside me.

'How soon and how easily our dream-life and our material life become so intermingled and so fused together that we can't quite tell which is which anymore,' he said.

'Mark Twain?' I asked. He nodded. 'My life's turning into a Mark Twain aphorism,' I observed.

'Mine already is,' he replied.

'I was hoping to bump into you again,' I said. 'I thought you might be able to shed some light on recent events.'

As I summarised the narrative you are reading up to this point, taking care not to divulge the full extent of my involvement, and omitting chapter eight entirely, I was struck by how unreal it all seemed and I could tell from Twain's uncomprehending reaction that my ill-defined suspicion of his complicity was unfounded.

'What makes you think I can shed some light on any of this?' he asked.

'The fact that coincidences are rare and yet here we are meeting on the same bench as this morning.'

'Who says coincidences are rare?'

'Me — and someone I met today.'

'Who?'

'A girl called Pardos.'

'And you agree with her?'

'Yes. Are you going to try and tell me that it's entirely coincidental that we've met here again?'

'No, it's not coincidental.'

'So, you've something to tell me?'

'Yes, but nothing that will shed any light on recent events.'

'What then?'

'Well, I returned with the hope of meeting you again,' he said, placing a hand on my knee. Realising his misjudgement from my reaction, he retrieved his hand and pocketed it, bringing an abrupt conclusion to a fraught-laden juncture by enquiring into the nature of my dream.

'I was about to be mauled by a black panther,' I said.

His reaction to this information was incredulous, as was my reaction to his reaction. He claimed (I use the word 'claimed' because, bearing in mind, once again, Pardos's assertion concerning the rarity of coincidences, this latest incidence immediately aroused my suspicions — but if it was not a coincidence, what was it?) that just prior to his stroll to this very park bench, he'd been immersed in an account of his namesake's travels in South East Asia, wherein passing reference had been made to the fact that, in Thailand, black panthers are considered by natives to be omens.

'I bet your girlfriend's black,' he said.

'She's not my girlfriend,' I said, not realising till I'd said it how much I yearned for her to be.

Later, unable to sleep, mulling over the accuracy of Twain's guess about Pardos's ethnic origin, I dug out Andy's last, undelivered, letter to you, as I had done on so many previous occasions. But whereas before I'd pored over this priceless, if somewhat worn and torn, artefact to wallow in a nostalgia for a lost utopia, this time I sought to clarify a particular aspect of this letter which had been troubling me since the previous day.

What was concerning me was the uneasy feeling that there was something familiar about the kidnapper's handwriting — a feeling that had only grown when I'd seen his letter reproduced on the front page of the paper that morning. Superficially, the kidnapper's and Andy's handwriting appeared markedly different — it would have been unusual for the calligraphy of an adult and a child to be strikingly similar — yet I fancied I could discern some fundamental similarities. So I sat with Andy's last letter to you in one hand and the kidnapper's first letter in my other, until I just about managed to convince myself that if Andy's handwriting had progressed into adulthood, then it would have approximated that of the kidnapper. But no sooner had I reached this conclusion than I recognised that a dispassionate third party would undoubtedly interpret it as no more than the wishful thinking of a remorseful father who'd failed to come to terms with the death of a beloved son — and yet ... it was because of my inability not to imagine the incredible (the possibility that Andy was somehow still alive and might even be the kidnapper) that I had thus far refrained from confessing to Pardos the full extent of my involvement in inciting the kidnapper's letter, for if it were ever to transpire that the incredible was revealed to be true, then how could I expose and condemn my own flesh and blood without first giving him the opportunity to explain his motives?

It was with such thoughts in mind that I slipped into another dream. I was on a beach, building a huge multi-turreted, seagull feather-flagged sandcastle with Andy, who wore a flesh-coloured eye patch under his sunglasses and looked about the age he would have been had he not committed suicide.

'I thought you were dead,' I said.

'You were meant to,' he replied, patting the sand with the back of his spade.

'Are you saying you deliberately deceived me?'

'Not at all,' he said.

'What then?'

'I'm telling you that *I* didn't write my suicide note.'

Although this news surprised me, because such a possibility hadn't occurred to me, it also struck me as obvious and I received it with a sense of relief, for, whatever ordeal it implied Andy had been subjected to, it meant that he hadn't written it with the malicious intention of deceiving me (the conclusion I had erroneously jumped to and which I couldn't bear to contemplate).

'Who did then?'

He hesitated from answering, gently patting the sand with the back of his spade. Impatient, I yanked it from him.

'You were abducted, weren't you?' I prompted. 'The kidnapper wrote the note and took you away.'

Andy confirmed my suspicions by his failure to deny them.

'Who was he?'

'I don't know his name. He insisted I call him "father".'

I returned the spade and he resumed patting the sand with it. 'Did he — hurt you?'

'Not really.'

'Did he say *why* he'd kidnapped you?'

'Yes — to punish you.'

'Me? Why would he want to punish me? What harm am I supposed to have done him?

'I don't know.'

'Did he say how he knew me?'

He shook his head.

'Where did he take you?'

'Palma.'

'How did you escape?'

'I didn't. He let me go.'

'Why?'

'I don't know.'

Just then, the tide rushed in, drowning our ineffectual moat and drowning our ramparts, sending a turret tottering into the retreating ripples.

'Why did you lie to me?' he asked.

'About what?'

'About angels and heaven.'

'To make it easier for you.'

'For me or for you?'

When I awoke from the dream I was suffused with a feeling that somehow everything was, and always would be, all right. This soon evaporated, to be supplanted by a prolonged and acutely felt fresh sense of loss. Uniquely, I could recall every detail of the dream, and this clarity made it feel real. It was only then, recounting the dream conversation with Andy, that it occurred to me that when his abductor had insisted he call him 'father', it could have been because he was a priest, rather than a deliberate attempt to usurp my position, as I had immediately interpreted it to mean.

Then, regarding anew the two letters in front of me, I was finally able to pinpoint what had struck me as familiar about the kidnapper's letter. By placing Andy's last letter to you behind the kidnapper's and holding them up to the light, I persuaded myself that the same hand had penned the letters. It wasn't the hand-writing that convinced me of this startling fact; the give-away was the wider than average space between each word, which was exactly the same on both letters.

chapter seventeen

the front page (2)

I ROLLED OUT OF BED, gulped down cornflakes, showered, shaved, shit and caught the 44 into work, immersed in the front page of the paper which, I could see, contained a reproduction of the kidnapper's second letter alongside an article on yesterday's developments, but I couldn't lift my eyes from the photograph dominating the front page to read them until well into my usual cramped commute.

The photograph showed two baby-faced teenage soldiers sharing a joke about the trophy the soldier on the right of the picture was holding up to display proudly to the photographer: the head of a third baby-faced teenage soldier; freshly decapitated with eyes open, surprised and not yet bereft of life.

This morbid fascination was interrupted when a grossly obese, sweaty schoolboy collapsed wheezing into the too-small space beside me, crushing me against the window as we swerved around a corner and I finally turned my attention to the article on the kidnapper. As usual, I'll reproduce it for you verbatim:

KIDNAP HOSTAGE TORTURED

Following yesterday's death threat, we have received a second anonymous letter from a kidnapper containing what has been confirmed to be a lens extracted from a human eye, prompting fears that the hostage has been tortured.

This second letter has been confirmed by expert graphologists to have been written by the author of the first, received the day before.

In the letter, addressed to our editor, John Kerr, the kidnapper writes that the publication of his first letter has momentarily spared the life of his hostage but warns that further refusal to condemn the views expressed in a letter about a book review we published earlier in the week (which seems to have prompted the kidnapping) will result in the death of the hostage, who the kidnapper asserts is a Mr Ian Thome.

The letters have sparked a nationwide manhunt for the kidnapper, with Chief Constable Allan Wallace of Strathclyde Police confirming that the case has been given top priority. A specialist unit has been assigned to the investigation, with additional resources being made available from Scotland Yard.

Whilst confirming that a team of investigators is actively pursuing a number of leads, Wallace yesterday expressed his firm belief that the hostage is still alive, stressing that his investigating team's top priority is to ensure his safe release at the earliest opportunity.

Whilst admitting that the true identity of the hostage was still open to question, and that it was unusual that no relatives had yet come forward to report an unexplained sudden disappearance of a family member, Wallace dismissed media speculation that the kidnap was little more than an elaborate hoax as 'unhelpful'.

He declined to speculate on how long it would take to secure the safe release of the hostage and appealed for the kidnapper to make contact with the police at the earliest opportunity to help resolve the situation before 'matters get out of hand'.

Wallace also appealed directly

to any members of the public who feel they might have some useful information which could lead to the identification of the hostage and/or kidnapper to come forward and make themselves known to the police.

He urged members of the public to carefully examine the kidnapper's letter and, if they feel they recognise the handwriting, to contact either this paper or their local police station immediately, with confidentiality guaranteed.

In what may turn out to be a significant revelation, our own investigative reporters tracked down Ian Thorne (the assumed hostage) at his home address in Glasgow's West End yesterday, prompting speculation that the kidnapper might have taken hostage the wrong person in a case of mistaken identity.

Whilst this interpretation of events remains unverified, recent research by terrorism expert Professor Paul Buchanan of the University of Glasgow revealing that botched kidnaps are not unknown, lends it some credence. Buchanan speculates that the kidnapper might only now be aware that he has taken the wrong person hostage and predicts the imminent safe release of his unfortunate victim.

Editor John Kerr has reiterated our steadfast stance to uphold the principles of free speech and outright condemnation of the kidnapper's tactics; a stance publicly endorsed by the First Minister and echoed by the opposition leaders when the matter was raised during First Minister's Questions at Holyrood yesterday afternoon.

We have set a £1000 reward for information leading to the safe release of the hostage and capture of the kidnapper. Any reader with information they think could lead to the identification of the hostage/ kidnapper can call our dedicated hotline on (0800) 439 439. Lines are now open. All calls are free and confidentiality is guaranteed.

See feature page 7

Page seven reiterated the events leading up to the kidnapping, which had been spelled out in the paper the day before. It also expanded on the front-page story, included a photograph of a bewildered Ian Thome on his doorstep and contained comments from human rights groups, church leaders and pro-life campaigners, all peddling their own particular perspectives but all, uniquely, united in their unequivocal condemnation of the kidnapper's actions.

The feature concluded with an open letter to the kidnapper from John Kerr offering a full page of the next day's paper to express his beliefs and defend his actions in writing in exchange for the safe return of the hostage.

I summoned my courage, as always, took a deep breath and squeezed into the crowded lift to the first floor and, unable to resist the temptation, before I even removed my coat and hat, stopped and glanced at the purple paperweight pinning down the pile of letters on my desk.

'Morning,' sighed Kirsty Baird, teacup in hand, on her way to the kitchen.

'Morning,' I obliged.

'How's the missus?' she asked.

'Fine,' I smiled. 'She's fine.'

An unmarked padded envelope, identical to the one received the previous morning, sat atop the letter pile. I opened it. Inside was a small, square blue velvet jewellery box, also identical to the one received the previous morning. In the midst of prising it open, I was interrupted by an explosion, triggering an instinctive attempt to shield my ears from the deafening detonation and my head from falling masonry. I fell to the floor and rolled under my desk to lessen the chances of impalement by the many and varied jagged lumps of hot metal or shards of glass rocketing around my immediate vicinity. It was from this cramped and lowly vantage point — with a fire alarm ringing inside my head — that I looked out upon a shattered office with a hailstorm cascading from its ceiling.

As I lay waiting for the hailstorm to abate, I took in the scene of devastation; an office whose ambience had been painstakingly designed by a team of consultants to maximise efficiency through space utilisation and staff productivity via the deployment of carefully co-ordinated complementary colour schemes and contemporary, German-designed ergonomic furniture and furnishings, reduced in a moment to a rubble of fractured workstations and shattered PCs. Remembering that I still held the jewellery box in my hand, I opened it to find a molar resting on a bed of white satin with a note attached to the underside of the box lid reading 'Actions speak louder than words' on one side and 'Eye for eye, tooth for tooth' on the other.

The alarm bell ringing inside my head shifted from being a tired cliché for the severe tinnitus from which I was suffering into an all-too-real fire alarm ringing by the fire escape. This was soon joined by a swelling cacophony of fire engine, ambulance and police car sirens, each clamouring for immediate attention. At the very moment I realised that the hailstones were fragments of glass — probably, I speculated, originating from Kerr's smoke aquarium — I was able to discern yet another ringing tone, this time from directly above my head. I listened to it for some time before feeling sufficiently secure to release one hand from protecting my fragile cranium to reach above and retrieve my phone.

'Intolerance will not be tolerated,' intoned a familiar electronically altered voice. 'Meet me at the flagpole at noon and I'll set free the hostage. Fail to appear and you'll read about his murder on tomorrow's front page. Come alone.'

chapter eighteen

letter bomb

A NUMBER OF JOURNALISTS were ferried to hospital suffering from injuries sustained by flying debris. The rumour circulating amongst staff as they evacuated the building in the immediate aftermath of the blast was that a letter bomb had been sent to John Kerr, who had chosen, fortuitously, to pay a visit to the gents immediately prior to its detonation.

As Dick and Hill pestered members of the emergency services for quotable information regarding the precise location of the detonation, the weight, size and design of the explosive device, the nature of injuries inflicted on people and damage caused to property, a traumatised Kerr and myself were summoned to our third board meeting in three days which, this time, had been convened in a conference room of the Holiday Inn. I immediately decided to keep the kidnapper's instruction to meet him at noon to myself for the time being.

The decor of the room may have differed from the paper's boardroom, but its atmosphere of intimidation was familiar, if intensified. Its occupants were the same as on the previous two occasions although, unusually, White Whiskers was already seated at the head of the table. I was pondering the significance of his uncharacteristically prompt attendance when he pounced on me.

'Is there any evidence linking the letter bomb to the kidnapper?' he growled.

I understood that the reason he was already seated was to catch me off guard before I had the chance to prepare a defence to his inquisition. I sensed that my survival depended upon my ability to respond to the forthright questions in the manner in which they were posed; with the conviction and confidence that are the hallmarks of honesty (no matter how dishonest my responses would be) rather than the obsequious yea-saying of his cardboard cut-out, pinstriped board of directors afraid to take any initiative for fear of the possible detrimental implications on the security of their pension plans.

'I believe so,' I said, tossing the jewellery box along the table.

'What's this?' he barked, regarding it with ill-disguised disdain.

'It's from the kidnapper,' I said. 'Open it.'

'Why is it that you receive gifts when your editor receives letter bombs?'

'It's not a gift. It's evidence. Open it up and read what it says.'

'*Actions speak louder than words*,' he read aloud, for the benefit of his board. 'And how does such a trite cliché constitute evidence?'

'Because it explains the motive,' I replied. 'The feature on page seven of this morning's paper concludes with a challenge to the kidnapper to defend his actions through words. The letter bomb was his response.'

'And the tooth?'

'Another sign to show he means business.'

The old man snapped the box shut and tossed it back to me.

'We followed your advice and look where it got us,' he said. 'It was your idea to reproduce the kidnapper's letter on the front page and seek to exploit the situation. It was your idea to print his second letter, to ridicule him and challenge him to respond. The result? We're lucky to be alive. As it is, the damage to our property will cost a fortune to repair. Will *you* foot the bill?'

'Not on the wages you pay me. No, I suspect your insurance will cover the cost. What's happened to circulation over the past two days? (I had overheard anecdotal evidence while people were milling around after the evacuation that sales had risen by a significant percentage.) What level of response have you had to your hotline? (I had also heard that the switchboard had already been inundated with calls.) You asked for my advice and I gave it — that's more than anybody else in this room was prepared to do. If you want to make me out to be the scapegoat — fine — but remember: nobody forced you to take my advice — you chose to take it yourself.'

White Whiskers' expression suggested that he hadn't anticipated such a combative response. Certainly, the pinstripes looked united in their desire to fire me with immediate effect. This was the unanimous decision they rapidly arrived at and proposed to Whiskers, who, his surprise having already started to subside, dismissed their bleating with a tired wave of a liver-spotted hand.

'You've got balls, kid,' he said, sounding for all the world like a capo in an American made-for-TV gangster movie. 'They're on the line.'

'I wouldn't have them anywhere else,' I said, surveying the room and rising to leave.

Pardos was waiting for me outside.

'We need to talk,' she said.

PART FOUR

mine oath

chapter nineteen

spell it out

WE RETURNED TO THE SPACE BAR. It was as bereft of customers as it had been the day before, so that there was no hiding from the tension that I found had sprung up between us. I interpreted this awkwardness as a sign that we'd arrived at a crucial juncture in our relationship. Neither of us seemed willing to attempt to ease the strain and cautiously chose our words before uttering them, trying to anticipate all the implications of each and every word and weighing up the most advantageous, or least disadvantageous, option open to us.

'I've got a present for you,' I said, handing her the jewellery box. She took it, opened it, closed it and deposited it in her pocket in a single motion.

'I'm going to ask you this one last time,' she said. 'D'you have something you want to tell me?'

'Yes,' I sighed.

'The truth?'

'The truth,' I said, raising my right hand with mock solemnity. 'This is mine oath. I swear to tell the truth, the whole truth, and nothing but the truth, so help me God.'

'D'you believe in God?'

'D'you believe in truth?'

'I see your trait's still intact.'

The waitress served our coffees. When she'd departed I finally confessed that both Ian Thome and Tom Haine were pseudonyms deployed by me. Pardos didn't seem at all surprised.

'Why didn't you tell me this yesterday?' she asked.

'I felt it was my responsibility — and mine alone — to try to resolve the situation I'd inadvertently created — '

' — You wanted to cover your tracks before you were caught and had to face the consequences,' she interrupted, savaging me with unanticipated disdain. Her tone revealed the cordiality of the day before as no more than a tactic in a strategy designed to deceive me into considering her an ally. I shuddered at the ease with which I'd fallen for her ploy.

'Why write under a pseudonym anyway?' she asked. 'Were you ashamed of what you'd written?'

'Why should I be ashamed? Yesterday you said you were captivated by it.'

'I said a lot of things yesterday,' she said, confirming that the charade of cordiality was over. 'Its title is, of course, an anagram of your name; can I take it that, since it's also written in the first person, the views voiced by the narrator are your own?'

'You can take it any way you want.'

'Well, let me tell you how I took it,' she said. 'I found its focus on logical analyses and its neglect of emotional concerns offensive. I thought it was written from a detached, hypothetical moral perspective untainted by the gory trauma of the close-up reality. I thought it failed to convey any real sense of the depth of the dilemma because it was written by someone who has never, and will never, have to confront that dilemma.'

Whilst I was wounded by the severity of her unexpected criticism, and suspected that it had been partly motivated by her own experience of the dilemma in question, I was more intrigued by its ring of familiarity.

'You sound just like Niamh — '

' — You're not the only one who can adopt pseudonyms,' she interrupted.

'You mean you're ... then who was the girl in the library?'

'A colleague.'

'But why would you — '

' — Let me spell it out for you,' she sighed, lighting a cigarette (I never knew she smoked, but then I never really knew her, did I?). 'The only lead in the unresolved Craig Liddell case was the name left in the hotel register — '

' — Toni Mahe,' I interrupted.

'Having wasted countless hours on fruitless research,' she continued as if she hadn't heard me, 'I'd eventually concluded that the name was fictitious, but significant — because of its very fictitiousness (no one would deliberately leave a randomly chosen name at a murder scene). I became convinced that the key to solving the case would only be found once I understood the significance of the pseudonym. It didn't take long from there to decipher the fact that the name was an anagram of "I am not he". At one point I took this literally and thought that this might be a clue to the sex of the murderer, but I later reverted to my original interpretation; that it was a way of confirming that the name Toni Mahe was a pseudonym. So — '

' — So you kept a look out for other pseudonyms which were variations of the "I am not he" anagram,' I interrupted. 'And when I published *Original Harm* under the pseudonym Tom Haine, you thought you might be on to something. Correct?'

'Correct.'

'And so — let me guess — you planted a scathing review under the pseudonym Niamh Toe to provoke a reaction from the murderer, in the hope that the recognition of your pseudonym would intrigue him. Correct?'

'Correct.'

'And, correct me if I'm wrong, when I then responded to your review using the pseudonym Ian Thome, you became convinced you'd found your man. Correct?'

'You're more astute than I gave you credit for,' she said.

'And when that response resulted in a kidnapping, all your suspicions were confirmed. Was I the prime suspect?'

'You were *a* suspect'

'I'm not anymore?'

'No.'

'Why not?'

'You're not murderer material,' she said, in a way that made it sound like an insult.

'Why not?'

'You know why not.' I wasn't at all sure that I did, but chose not to pursue the matter further.

'And yesterday, when you said that you'd been in touch with the publisher, Tina Home, that was a fishing expedition designed to prompt my admission that I'd written and published *Original Harm* myself, correct?'

'Correct.'

'So what happens now?' I asked.

'I want you to tell me everything you know about The Amino,' she said.

'They're fictional,' I replied.

'They're a fact,' she insisted. 'And you christened them.'

'As far as I'm aware they exist only within the pages of *Original Harm.*'

'If only that were true,' she sighed. 'But we know that the kidnapper, whoever he is, is a member. We also know that you invented their ideology. How d'you explain that?'

I shrugged and said, 'Sometimes life imitates art.'

'Now where have I heard that before?' she answered, feigning forgetfulness. 'Oh yes, the kidnapper deposited that little cliché inside yesterday's jewellery box.'

'That's just a coincidence.'

'I thought I'd already told you — I don't believe in coincidences.'

'That doesn't mean they don't exist.'

She sighed.

'D'you think Ian Thome's kidnapper killed Craig Liddell?' I asked.

'Yesterday you told me you'd no kids,' she said, ignoring my question.

'I didn't tell you anything,' I corrected, 'I shook my head.'

'But you have a son.'

'*Had*. He's dead.'

'You know that for a fact?'

This question reinforced my growing inkling that the tragedy I'd long since resigned myself to accept as incontrovertible fact, might not be true, and that my fantasy (that — somehow, some-day — the incontrovertible fact would be revealed to have been founded upon a series of erroneous assumptions by a simple explanation for Andy's disappearance which, once it had been uttered, seemed perfectly plausible so that I wondered why it had never occurred to me before) might well be true.

The waitress removed our empty coffee cups with a clumsy clatter and a wipe of the tabletop as Pardos sought to second-guess my thoughts.

'Is there anything *you* want to tell *me*?' I said, all trace of irony drained from my tone. She changed the topic, prolonging my suffocation.

'Does anyone else know about your deployment of pseudo-nyms?' she asked.

'Not that I know of — apart from Chris.'

'Chris?'

'The Crossword Compiler — but he's not the kidnapper, if that's what you're thinking.'

'You know that for a fact?'

I took a deep breath and it occurred to me that Pardos thought I was shielding his identity from her.

'As good as,' I said.

'Anyone else?'

'Not that I can think of.'

'Think carefully now. We don't have much time.'

I hesitated a moment before answering, weighing up the pros and cons of revealing the kidnapper's demand that I meet him at the flagpole at noon before deciding, finally, to keep schtum for now.

'For the past decade I've had way too much,' I said, glancing at my watch. It was 11:45am. 'Now I don't have enough.'

I rose to leave then hesitated once more. There were a thousand things I wanted to say to her but didn't know how or where to begin.

PART FIVE

i'm on heat

chapter twenty

the present tense

IT WAS PROBABLY THE GLIMPSE Pardos caught of me hailing
down a taxi that alerted her to the fact that something was afoot
but by then it was already too late for her to attempt to follow
me so, instead — and I only discovered this when I read about
it later in an extended article by-lined to Dick and Hill — she
hailed her own taxi and directed it to my home address where
she searched my flat for clues to the identity of the kidnapper.

Just how she gained entry, given that there was no evidence
of any force having been used, I don't know. And just how she
deduced that any such clues might be gleaned from a cursory
examination of my flat I'm not sure either, but I suspect that
proficiency in deduction was a fundamental requirement of her
occupation and she no doubt had an array of skills and tech-
niques unknown to me at her disposal.

Certainly on this occasion her deduction had proved to be
accurate. Pardos had discovered an abundance of clues, including a manuscript of *Original Harm*. Of more interest to her,
though, were the two letters I'd reread in the pre-dawn hours
of that same day, searching desperately for clues; together with
a pile of letters she discovered stacked randomly on my bookshelf from a long extinguished epistolary friendship which (she
deduced from their quantity) spanned an extensive period.

It was then that her ever-dependable hunch, that sixth sense required by all detectives, private or otherwise, if they ever hope to bring a case to a satisfactory conclusion, made its presence felt and Pardos sensed that the solution to uncovering the identity of the kidnapper lay somewhere in this unsorted stack of letters. Whilst her instinct was to file them according to their dates, so that she could examine them sequentially, she found herself distracted by a compelling sense of urgency so that, whilst seeking to establish some semblance of chronological order to the correspondence, she stole intermittent glances at certain passages of various letters out of sequence if the subject matter intrigued her sufficiently.

In one letter, written in the handwriting of a child still endeavouring to master the art of the written word, Pardos found herself captivated by the unbridled excitement of its juvenile author enthusing about *Alice in Wonderland*. In the very next letter she read (surely not coincidentally), an adult hand extolled the virtues of *Crime and Punishment* with an equally eager conviction that seemed almost childlike in its lack of cynicism. Their dates revealed that the second letter had been penned nearly a decade after the first and their signatures (although differing superficially as a consequence of substantially improved handwriting skills over the intervening years) revealed that both letters had been penned by the same hand.

As Pardos became immersed in the multitude of letters rhapsodising about a variety of subjects — TV programmes, music and books, lots of books — she soon found herself to be infected by the contagious *joie de vivre* that characterised the correspondence. Reading the letters rekindled in her a capacity for enchantment. But no sooner had this capacity begun to warm her than it was extinguished once and for all by a gust of suspicion that swept her from her reverie back to the present tense. The catalyst of extinction was the mid-section of a letter untainted by the pervasive naivety, striking, instead, a sour note. As ever, I'll reproduce it for you verbatim:

... because the fact of the matter is that I understand the way Tom Sawyer thinks about things better than I understand anyone else I know — including you. I thought I knew you. I thought you knew me. But when I read what you thought of my novel A Halo Ring Rim I realised that neither of us had ever really known the other.

I know it would be pointless to try to counter your criticisms (except to say that the eyeball-slitting scene was intended as an homage to, not a 'rip-off' of, Buñuel, just as the molar cufflinks were intended as an allusion to, rather than a 'parodic travesty' of, Gatsby's Meyer Wolfshiem) because I know that all you did was tell me what you really thought and that I can ask you for no more.

It was then that her gaze fell upon the bookshelf where the very journal you're reading now lay open at its last entry — the events described a few pages back — my meeting with Mark Twain, my dream about Andy and my comparing of Andy's last letter with the kidnapper's.

As soon as she finished reading this last entry, Pardos rushed from the flat and sprinted to Queen's Park as fast as she could.

chapter twenty-one

her word against mine

IT WAS EN ROUTE to my rendezvous with the kidnapper as I sat
wringing my hands in the back seat of the taxi that I realised that
the flicker of hope I'd dared not permit myself to contemplate
all those years, yet had proven so resolutely inextinguishable, had
finally been fulfilled: Andy was alive. I could feel it. He might be
a kidnapper (if so, there had to be extenuating circumstances)
but he was my son and he was *alive* and I was about to be reu-
nited with him after all these long, drawn-out years.

As I speculated on just how this miracle of resurrection had
come to pass, the scenario I sketched assumed the following
indefinite shape: grief-stricken at the untimely demise of his
mother, Andy had instinctively sought to apportion blame. I
remember reading an article in the paper by a renowned psy-
chiatrist explaining that such a response was to be expected as
it provided the bereaved with a convenient fall-guy towards
which they could direct the full vent of their remorse. It is
a recognised way of coping with the shock of bereavement
and, in most cases, over time, the need to apportion blame
will subside alongside the shock until the stark fact of death is
assimilated and there is an acceptance that no amount of blame
apportionment will alter that fact. No doubt Andy blamed me

for Lisa's death. Given the circumstances — I was convenient and there was really no one else in the frame — I suppose this was to be expected. What was perhaps unexpected was that, instead of affording his grievance the time and space to subside and learning to reconcile himself to the fact of his mother's death, Andy had acted on it immediately (perhaps this reaction too should have been anticipated, given his tender years — he was only seven at the time — which must have made his grief seem unbearable) and sought, instead, to avenge her and exact revenge upon me by faking his own death; an action which must have provided him with an instant outlet for his grief and displaced it on to me. And if Andy had blamed me *then*, in the immediate aftermath of his mother's death, had he nurtured his hate for me throughout the duration of his formative years, waiting for the right time to exact his revenge? And if so, then what was it about now that made it the right time? Could it be connected to the publication of *Original Harm*?

What if Lisa had indoctrinated Andy's malleable young mind with poisonous lies about me? Lies? What lies? And why would she do such a thing? Perhaps she had acted on a notion that she had a duty to inform her son of the truth — she had always felt the need to confess, even when it seemed obvious that only harm could ever come from a particular confession — whatever she considered the truth to be. For Lisa the truth was absolute, whereas I constantly questioned her conception of it and disputed her version of it. For me, the truth depended on which particular version of it you chose to believe, by which I mean that it could be reduced to a question of favouring one person's word over another's.

And then it hit me. Of course! It seemed so obvious now! Everything fell into place. I knew *exactly* the 'truth' Lisa had spoon-fed Andy and I could pinpoint the precise time and location of her premeditated poisoning of his notion of me only all too clearly.

It would have been during the afternoon of the day of her death in Majorca that she'd have decided to confess the events of Andy's conception to him. It's only now that I can begin to realise the significance of that afternoon (given the subsequent events of that day, it is perhaps understandable that I should have overlooked it). Sprawled out on Port de Soller's Repic beach, Lisa sat tucked away beneath the shade of an umbrella, with us but apart, under duress and no doubt seething at me for insisting that she spend some time with her family, engrossed in *The Story of O*, myself stealing glances at a topless trio of frolicking *Fräuleins* tossing a Day-Glo yellow frisbee to and fro amidst the surf, when Andy stopped patting his sandcastle with the back of his spade to interrupt the silence with one of his queries. Where, he wondered, apropos of nothing in particular — perhaps a toddler had tottered past, or a sun-stroked baby had squawked for some of its mother's milk — did babies come from? For once I'd forsaken my parental duties by opting to escape for a refreshing dip in the sea, leaving Lisa to answer his enquiry. It was then, I realise now, that she had chosen to poison him with her version of the truth.

Lisa was adamant that, without exception, truth was the best policy. The notion that it might be in Andy's best interests if she were to censor any aspect of the truth would not have occurred to her. Lisa would regard such censorship as an ill-conceived allowance made for juvenile sensibilities and a serious dereliction of her duty. Of this I was certain. In all matters, Lisa addressed Andy as an equal. No doubt my flight from Andy's enquiry would have infuriated her. I'm sure that, whilst I was busy bathing in the Mediterranean, Lisa was giving Andy a graphic account of the act of his conception and sparing him no blushes.

'You were born as a result of your dad raping me,' she would have said, matter-of-factly.

She always dropped her bombshells that way, as if she was making small talk and her revelations were no more provocative

132

than everyday observations about the weather. It was as though she set out to pre-empt and undermine the anticipated shocked response from the recipients of her surprises so that her deadpan delivery led them to question the appropriateness of such a reaction. That's how she would have told Andy. I can hear her voice.

'One night, when he was blind drunk, your dad forced himself upon me against my will,' she would have said, 'and, though I struggled against him and pleaded with him to stop, he was stronger than me and when he punched me I realised that further resistance was futile.'

It's imperative that you believe me when I insist that, though this might well have been Lisa's truth, it was, nevertheless, a travesty of the truth. It was false in every respect.

The fact of the matter was that, on the night in question — a Friday — I arrived home later than usual after a particularly stressful week (a by-election campaign had just started and the postbag had begun to bulge with mountainous volumes of the usual petty and parochial party political propaganda for me to wade through in the forlorn hope of uncovering a letter written by an author expressing an independent, coherent opinion) laden with a couple of bottles of my favoured Jacob's Creek Cabernet Sauvignon purchased from Oddbins en route. Whilst it is true that, on the night in question, Lisa chose not to join me in the consumption of these delectable bottles of South Eastern Australian vintage 1998, it is equally true that I only opened one of the two bottles and, having sampled several glasses throughout a hearty two-course meal, I sipped at the remainder of the bottle throughout the rest of the evening as I sat in my worn armchair reading a book that Lisa had leant me, so that, though relaxed, I was not intoxicated.

I mention the book Lisa had lent me because I believe it had a significant part to play in the subsequent events of the evening in question. I remember it well. It left a lasting impression on me. It was called *The Image* and, since it traversed the blurred boundary between the erotic and the pornographic, I'd fancied that Lisa had lent it to me with the precise intention of arousing me with a view to precipitating some sexual congress later that evening. This was at a time when we were still sexually active. Little did I know then that this was to be our last sexual encounter.

In retrospect it could be argued with some validity that I'd misread Lisa's intentions in lending me the book — she herself was adamant that this was indeed the case — but then, can everything not be reinterpreted in a different light under the beneficial glare of hindsight? Nevertheless, I still did not force her against her will. Although perhaps slower than usual to respond to my advances, my fumbling fingers had met with no resistance and her thighs had duly parted as wide and as welcoming as ever before.

As for Lisa's claim that I punched her, this was no more than a deliberately misleading gross exaggeration of a playful slap; a slap, moreover, which she herself was in the habit of urging me to deliver but which my reticence meant that I was only ever able to provide half-heartedly.

In fact, now that I think about it, not only had Lisa urged me to slap her on the night in question, she'd insisted that I verbally abuse her too. It seemed to excite her.

'Call me a whore,' she'd whispered, squeezing me. I concurred.

'Call me a bitch,' she'd demanded, manipulating me.

'I'm on heat,' she'd said, swallowing me.

Distracted from my thoughts by the taxi driver swerving to avoid a pensionable pedestrian who had wandered inadvertently into his path, I felt I understood the motive behind Andy's hatred for me all these years. I could comprehend his insatiable lust for revenge. I could hear Lisa prompting it with her poisonous truth.

'Later, when your dad discovered that I was pregnant with you, he flew into a rage and demanded that I have an abortion,' I can hear her tell him.

'When I refused, he hit me so hard that I had to hide the bruise on my cheek under a thick layer of foundation for a week.'

Yes, that's what she'd done. That explained everything. She'd force-fed Andy her own twisted truth and poisoned him against me.

The taxi screeched to a halt and I sprinted up the steep hill to the flagpole at the top of Queen's Park.

Finally I felt I was beginning to comprehend a connection between *Original Harm* and why Andy had reacted to it in such an extreme and irrational manner. All these years he'd thought that I'd sought to have him aborted and now here I was, dedicating a book sympathetic towards abortion to him. How he must despise me! How anxious I was to enlighten him about his mother's lies and to convey to him some sense of the ecstasy of relief that surged through me now I knew he was alive. How anxious I was to explain to him how much he meant to me and that, now that I had him back and had been granted a second chance, this time around I'd never let him go. I had to put him right on what had really happened between Lisa and me. I had to tell him the truth and then maybe we could start to explore ways to resolve the predicament within which we'd ensnared each other.

It was Andy, I now realised, who had transformed The Amino from fiction into fact. It was Andy who was the kidnapper. I knew I had to reach him before Pardos. Reflecting on my last conversation with her, it seemed clear to me now that she already suspected him.

As I approached the flagpole, I noticed Mark Twain waiting for me on the bench and all my speculations that I had just delineated so diligently started to unravel. Perhaps Andy wasn't the kidnapper, after all? And, if not, did that mean that he *was* dead? Was Mark Twain the kidnapper? Perhaps he was Andy's messenger?

This latter speculation seemed the most plausible when, without words, Mark Twain rose as I approached and beckoned me to follow him. It was only then that I remembered presenting Andy with a copy of *The Adventures of Huckleberry Finn* for his seventh birthday. It had been a favourite book of mine ever since I'd been sent it as a childhood present myself, and I'd duly presented it to Andy with an inscription expressing the hope that it bring him as much pleasure as it had brought me.

Twain led me round behind the flagpole and along a muddy path to Hill 60, through mature oak trees to allotments where a sprawl of broken-windowed greenhouses and assorted storm-damaged sheds bordered rows of cultivated vegetables.

'Are you the messenger?' I asked him. He nodded and pointed to a ramshackle shack constructed from rusted sheets of corrugated tin located in the far corner then turned to leave.

'Is this goodbye?' I asked. Again he nodded. 'You never did tell me your real name,' I said. I don't know why — perhaps, as a consequence of my mounting trepidation, I was seeking to stall my meeting with Andy — but I felt compelled to strike up a conversation with him.

'No, I didn't,' he said, turning to leave again, before changing his mind and calling, 'Guy Fall.'

'So, why the pseudonym?'

He shrugged. 'You'll need to ask "him".'

'Who's "him"?'

He shrugged again. 'He never told me his name and, having asked once, I learned quickly not to ask again.'

I watched him disappear over the brow of the hill then approached the shack with caution. Swinging open the creaking door, I peered inside. It was dark and stank of stale cabbage, bruised Brussels sprouts, turnips and other rotting vegetables.

'Andy?' I heard my voice asking in anticipation. There was no reply but I heard a shuffle in the shadows. I cleared my throat and tried again.

'Andy?' I repeated, louder this time.

There was a muffled cough and then I heard a gruff voice from within the midst of the darkness:

'Andrew's dead.'

PART SIX

a tin home

chapter twenty-two

character assassination

'How d'you know?' I asked.

'I've read his suicide note,' said the disembodied voice.

'Have you seen his body?'

'No.'

'Then how d'you *know* he's dead?'

The voice coughed and I listened to its laboured breathing.

'I don't have to see his body to know he's dead. I've read his suicide note. You know he's dead too.'

'I do?'

'Yes, you do. You might not want to admit it to yourself; you might try to kid yourself that the fact that his body was never found means that somehow he's still alive — and, knowing how your mind works, you've probably conjured up some fantastical scenario in your head to explain to yourself that Andrew's the kidnapper — but, deep down, you and I both know that he's dead.'

The brutal truth of these words slashed open my scars of grief to lay bare the wounds I'd hoped had healed over but which were now revealed to have been festering all this time.

'Speak for yourself,' I said in a last ditch attempt at denial. 'Who *are* you anyway? And what makes you think you know how my mind works?'

The forced breathing stopped and a figure marched with precision from the shadows into the murky light as if obeying a command. His erect posture, standing to attention with puffed-out chest and chin aloft, expressionless face staring me straight in the eye, as if presenting itself for inspection, suggested a military bearing. He held my gaze for an instant before jerking his head involuntarily. This twitch, which I interpreted as a physical manifestation of some psychological torment, was to recur at irregular intervals throughout the remainder of our conversation. Dishevelled and clothed in threadbare military fatigues, he wore a worn blue beret and a flesh-coloured eye patch. Despite his attempt at striking an imposing presence, there was no disguising the fact that he had been through the wars and was in a poor physical and mental condition. I was reminded of the recent spate of photographs and reports of a brutally executed campaign of ethnic cleansing that had so disturbed me and sensed that the individual before me had been living what I'd been reading.

'I'm the kidnapper — ' he declared, letting slip a slight American twang that triggered a desperate search for recognition in my head.

' — I thought as much,' I interrupted.

' — And the hostage,' he finished, catching me off guard.

As soon as he spoke these words, there was a distinct degeneration in his demeanour. It was as if he'd relieved himself of an unbearable burden and forsaken the willed maintenance of a facade of vitality. His forced breathing resumed, he twitched several times in rapid succession and started to shrivel before my eyes, his back becoming bent and bowed, his hands trembling. I watched this metamorphosis impassively as I struggled to comprehend the implications of his revelation.

'I'm not sure I understand,' I managed eventually, inviting him to spell it out for me.

He flashed a grotesque grin, with the express purpose, I suspect

140

in retrospect, of revealing to me the bloody gap in his gum from where his missing molar had only recently been uprooted.

'What don't you understand?'

'Anything.'

'You really don't know who you are, do you?' he said.

I certainly didn't understand this remark — it struck me as platitudinous — but I was about to.

'Let me enlighten you.'

'What's your name?' I interrupted once more in an attempt to regain some measure of control over the proceedings.

'Liam,' he said, coughing, then, noticing my hesitation, he added, 'There was a time, long ago, when we exchanged confidences on a regular basis. *That's* what makes me think I know how your mind works. I can read you like a book.'

Not for the first time since he'd stepped from the shadows did I find myself at a loss for words. I searched in vain for an appropriate response to this revelation. Before me stood my confidant. I had confided in him without reservation from my childhood, throughout my adolescence and on into my adulthood. I believed him when he said he knew how my mind worked. I believe you can tell a lot about someone by reading their writing but I had read plenty of his letters and I hadn't foreseen this turn of events. Hadn't he confided in me?

'Of course I had,' he said, as if I'd spoken my thoughts aloud, or as if he really had been reading me like a book, 'but you were always too wrapped up in yourself to notice or care.'

I looked at him and realised that I had no idea how his mind worked or how I should respond to his revelation; that his accusation was probably accurate; that I probably had failed to reciprocate the attention he had afforded the barrage of perpetually self-propagating trivial torments with which I had bombarded him.

If I accepted my guilt in this regard then something told me that I was due to be sentenced. I could detect a menacing hostility emanating from him and, trying to remember the circumstances in which our correspondence had concluded, and which one of us had ended it, determined to proceed with caution.

'Your wounds are self-inflicted?' I asked.

'I lost my eye in combat,' he said. 'After some persuasion the surgeon let me keep the lens as a memento, but, yes, I extracted my tooth myself.'

'I can't think why you'd do something like that.'

'You wouldn't be here if you could,' he said. 'I did it to attract your attention.'

'Seems a bit extreme.'

'Sometimes extremes are necessary,' he replied.

'Well, you wanted my attention and you've got it,' I said. 'Why d'you want it?'

'To tell you all about me and you.'

'What about me and you?'

'What d'you think happened to me and you?' he asked. I shrugged, trying again to remember just how our correspondence had concluded.

'We grew up,' I offered.

'Is that it?' he asked.

I shrugged again.

'You really don't know who you are, do you?' he said again, the remark sounding more menacing and less trite second time around. I sighed, becoming disorientated by the opaque circularity of the conversation.

'Enlighten me,' I said, resigning from any further attempt to steer the roundabout course of our discourse.

'I will,' he replied. 'That's why you're here, but be warned because, in doing so, I'll undoubtedly damage irrevocably all the preconceived certainties of the autobiography you've been re-running and revising in that tape loop in your head, according to which, your life's divided into two acts: before and after the tragedies.

'Before the tragedies, according to your autobiography, your life was progressing largely as planned, following the upward trajectory of a narrative arc, heading straight towards the Holy Grail of happiness, that peaked and plateaued shortly after you became a father. The catalyst of this arc was Lisa, whom, for a while, you loved enough to consider her welfare as a matter of equal importance to your own. At the height of your infatuation with Lisa, it might even be true to say that you went so far as to defer the attainment of a portion of your own happiness in favour of hers — something you'd never contemplated before, or countenanced since. This unprecedented period concluded with the birth of Andrew, with whom Lisa was unable to compete for your hard-won affection.

'When Andrew arrived on the scene Lisa found herself cast aside — she'd delivered your son and heir and now found herself surplus to your requirements — and you diverted all your care and attention towards him. You found it easier to devote yourself to Andrew than to Lisa because you regarded him as an extension of yourself. Andrew became your *raison d'être*. You loved him unconditionally because he was your own flesh and blood. You even fancied that he granted you immortality. It was the thought of the death sentence of life with which, you and I both know — believe me I've got the mountains of documentation to back me up — you were unable to come to terms. You were and are petrified by the notion of coming to a full stop — a "dead end", you once called it — and, for a while at least, Andrew allowed you to bask in the illusion of your own immortality; an illusion that was shattered by his tragic suicide.

'Your arc of triumph plummeted in the aftermath of the tragedy of Lisa and Andrew's suicides, which signalled the culmination of Act One of your autobiography. According to your revised and self-edited version of events, you had had everything — a woman who loved you and whom you loved and a devoted son on whom you doted — only to lose it all in the space of a single day. Fate had conspired to strip you bare of all hope of happiness and condemn you to endure the remainder of your days wading through a quagmire of everlasting remorse. How could you ever hope to cope with such a dismal prospect?

'You coped by doing what you always did when confronted by your torments, trivial or otherwise — you wrote about them. They never seemed so insurmountable once they'd been transformed into words on a page where you could control and manipulate them — erase and edit, consider or consign them to a drawer — as you saw fit. So Act Two saw you start to exploit your torments as source material for a book. And you distorted them, perhaps unintentionally at first, but soon you discovered that you enjoyed the distortion and so you set about systematically exaggerating and embroidering the facts into fiction, rewriting your autobiography into an auto*hagi*ography in which you cast yourself in the role of martyr, an innocent tortured by the cruel twists of fate — '

' — *Enough!*' I interrupted. I couldn't bear to listen to his character assassination a moment longer. 'What gives you the right to judge me?' I demanded, frustrated by the ease with which he, an obviously deranged and quite possibly dangerous (certainly to himself) fantasist, had contrived to seize the moral high ground. 'What does any of this have to do with you anyway?'

'I've got every right to judge you,' he replied in a tone which suggested that he'd anticipated just this interruption, 'because this has everything to do with me. Your autobiography's a work of fiction, testament not to the tragic truth but to the vividness of your imagination and the pathos of your self-deception. The premises upon which it's founded — your love for Lisa and Andrew — are false — '

' — That's a lie!' I protested, but he proceeded without hesitation.

'Lisa never loved you, and you never loved her — '

' — That's a lie!'

'Is it? Explain to me just how you can beat and rape someone you purport to love?'

' — That's a lie!' I ejaculated for a third time.

'And as for Andrew: you claim to have been devoted to him, but the fact is that you wanted him aborted for fear that he would take your place in Lisa's affections — not realising that she never truly loved you anyway — and you harboured a festering resentment against him for having displaced you ever since — '

' — That's a lie!'

'The only thing you loved in Andrew was your reflection and the intimation of immortality he represented.'

This really was too much.

'Lies! All lies!' I proclaimed as, unable to contain my fury at his pseudo-psychobabble any longer, I lunged at him. He evaded my clumsy attack all too easily and, with a single strike, sent me careening across the room to crash against a bookcase and slump to the floor with books tumbling around me. I was disconcerted to discover that the books were all identical. They were all copies of *Original Harm*.

'Lies, all lies,' I mumbled beneath my breath.

'It's your autobiography that's the lie,' he maintained.

'And what about yours?' I hissed. 'What's *your* story?'

'At last,' he said, in a sarcastic tone. 'I was beginning to wonder whether you'd ever get round to enquiring after me.'

'I'm enquiring now,' I said, cradling my bruised and battered face in my hands. 'Do *you* know who *you* are?'

'Thanks for asking,' he said. 'I do — though I admit there was a time when I wasn't quite so sure —'

' — When was that?'

'When you stopped replying to my letters — those letters might not have meant much to you but they meant a great deal to me. I'd grown to depend on them — they gave me something to look forward to and, until you stopped sending them, they told me who I was: I was your confidant. I felt privileged to be the sole recipient of your candid confessions and, secure in the status this prerogative afforded me, the regular flow of your correspondence gave me sufficient self-confidence to inspire my first steps towards self-exploration until I learned to raise my line of vision from contemplation of my navel to contemplation of a vista crowded with possibilities. I took succour from your candour and sought to emulate it through my own experiments in self-expression, resulting in *A Halo Ring Rim*, my one and only attempt at writing a *roman-à-clef*. Your response to these overtures? You cut dead all lines of communication.'

I was unsure what, exactly, he was talking about. It sounded to me as if he was skirting around an issue he felt compelled to impart; as if he hoped that by broaching it indirectly, I might be able to infer his meaning without forcing him into the awkward position of having to divulge it explicitly. If this was his hope, then it was in vain.

Despite the accusation that culminated this preliminary bout of soul-baring confession, his voice had grown more reflective and less vindictive and I felt obliged to modulate my own accordingly.

'I'm not sure I follow,' I said.

'I thought you might find it difficult,' he said, 'but you weren't interested in my torments then, so you'll understand why I'm not predisposed to spell them out for you now. Suffice to say that they weren't as trivial or as commonplace as your own. It's what happened after your letters stopped arriving that should concern you.'

'What happened?'

'I decided that words are no substitute for action.'

'Meaning?'

'Meaning I felt I needed to meet you in person.'

'Me? Why?'

'I needed to clarify something with you.'

'What?' I asked.

'It doesn't matter now.'

'I'd like to know.'

'It doesn't matter now,' he repeated, in a tone that told me that any attempt to discuss this particular matter further would prove futile. His obfuscation was becoming exasperating. I sighed with frustration.

'So what happened,' I asked. 'You didn't find me, so you returned home?'

'Not immediately.'

'What d'you mean, "not immediately"?'

'I mean "not immediately". Which part of "not immediately" don't you understand? I didn't find *you* — but I found Lisa.'

'You knew Lisa?'

'Biblically,' he said, just like that, then, tangentially, 'D'you know what day it is today?'

'No,' I said, still trying to figure out whether he meant what I thought he meant by his confirmation that he had known Lisa.

'It's the tenth anniversary of your tragedies,' he said. 'You'd have thought that date might have etched itself in your memory — '

'What does the anniversary of "my tragedies" have to do with you?'

'Everything.'

'What d'you mean, "everything"?'

'I mean everything: your tragedies are mine.'

'What d'you mean?'

'I've just told you that I *knew* Lisa in the biblical sense — what d'you think I mean?'

It took me a moment to digest the inference of this taunt and a moment longer for me to react to it. I sprung to my feet and lunged at him for a second time, regaining consciousness to find myself crumpled in a heap with blood dripping from my nose and mouth and a metaphorical sledgehammer lodged in my head.

I became aware of his voice talking in a detached monotone that sounded as if he was reciting a text he'd rehearsed from memory like a second-rate actor who'd rote-learned lines written in a foreign language.

'... I blamed myself for driving you away and recoiled from any further attempts at self-discovery,' he was saying, as if explaining himself to himself as much as to me, 'but I found myself driven by an irrational need for your approval; a need which magnified during the protracted period of your failure to respond to my words. This lack of *any* feedback unsettled me more than a negative rejoinder might have done. I could only conclude that you deemed my writing unworthy of acknowledgement. But I felt my words deserved that at least, so that, once I'd resigned myself to the notion that no reaction was forthcoming, I flew here to demand one in person.

'When I arrived at your apartment, straight from the airport, you'd already left for work and, once I'd introduced myself, Lisa invited me in to share the pot of tea she'd just brewed. I couldn't help but notice that I'd interrupted her reading — *Irene's Cunt* lay open on the kitchen table — and so I offered to leave and return that evening, but she insisted that I stay. She was like that, wasn't she? She had that effortless ability to put people at ease in any given social situation. I always envied her that. She told me all about you. In retrospect, I suspect that I'd fallen in love with her right there and then. I didn't have the vocabulary to describe the feelings I was feeling then, but she seemed to breathe life into me, like an author who creates a fictional character with such skill that he seems alive to the reader — like the way you once wrote to me that you had to keep reminding yourself that Tom Sawyer was fictional and that each time you remembered this fact, you felt as though you'd lost a friend — '

' — Hence this Guy Fall character adopting Mark Twain as a namesake?' I interrupted, it only just dawning on me.

Liam nodded. 'You revealed your weakness for pseudonyms some time ago — what better pseudonym to give *my* messenger, not Andy's, than that adopted by the author of our shared favourite fictional character of our distant, innocent childhood? And what better pseudonyms to precipitate this meeting than variations of the "I am not he" anagram adopted by your good, or should that be bad, self?'

When this offhand remark met with nothing other than silence and an expression of perplexed puzzlement from myself, Liam sighed impatiently and, as if speaking to a dim-witted child, said, 'I am Toni Mahe. And Noa...'

'*You* murdered Craig Liddell?' I asked incredulously.

'Who else could it have been?'

'But why?' I asked, still uncomprehending.

'As a means to an end. To start the ball rolling. That and the fact that — not that you even noticed — but, years ago, he did a hatchet job on *A Halo Ring Rim*. I've been nurturing my wrath ever since, so, when the opportunity presented itself, Liddell elected himself as the perfect candidate to draw your attention — and *I* did a hatchet job on *him*. As I said: sometimes extremes are necessary. As soon as *Original Harm* was published, I recognised it as an unsubtle plagiarised parody of *A Halo Ring Rim*, and that you were the author writing under a pseudonym. So I adopted the nom de plume Toni Mahe to do the dirty deed, with the intention of gaining your attention, forgetting just how slow on the uptake you can be at times.' This latter remark was imparted with a tone of almost wistful affection, which somehow made it all the more menacing.

'Then, later, I thought I'd give you a second chance to put the pieces of the puzzle together, so I phoned your crossword puzzle colleague using the pseudonym Noah Time and, finally, we began to bring matters to a satisfactory conclusion.

'Anyway, to get back to what I was saying before I was so rudely interrupted, Lisa fleshed me out and I suspect she did the same to you.

'That evening, as I returned to meet you — Lisa and I had arranged it as a surprise for you — I found myself hesitating in the hallway outside your door with my fist raised, ready, but somehow unable, to knock. I finally realised why our correspondence had come to an end. With Lisa fleshing you out, why would you ever have need of me? As you said yourself a few moments ago, you felt you'd outgrown the need for me. Lisa had usurped me. As I stood there, I understood this and so I turned on my heels and hailed a taxi to the airport.

'When I reached home there was a letter waiting for me from Lisa wondering what had happened to me and whether or not I thought that she should inform you of my visit. I instructed her not to. I told her that your correspondence with me had concluded, thanked her for her hospitality and wished her a happy future with you. She responded by thanking me for my kind words, wished me well and, as far as I was concerned, that was that. I returned to my studies and tried to forget all about you and Lisa. Then, about a year later, I received a letter from her which made me feel like a character in a book who'd been reassigned a different identity and pitched headfirst into the midst of a plot he no longer recognised.

'Lisa's letter informed me that she was a mother and that I was a father of a baby boy. She apologised upfront for burdening me with this confession but sought to justify it to herself by arguing that her conscience compelled her to inform me of the truth. She stressed that she wasn't seeking any ongoing financial commitment from me to help her raise our son and begged that I do nothing about the situation because you'd already jumped to the conclusion that the child was your own and she'd no intention of enlightening you as to the truth. She'd enclosed several blurred Polaroids of a cherubic baby boy who, conceivably, resembled myself. But it was not these photos that convinced me of her startling claim — it was her absolute conviction that you were not the father.'

Liam's revelations seemed to me to be designed to provoke a further violent reaction from me and so I resolved to deny him that satisfaction. Instead, I listened impassively. I felt detached from the story he was telling. Instead of enraging me, which, I knew, was his intention, I let his words wash over me.

My own serenity at this juncture contrasted starkly with Liam's now agitated state. Whereas earlier his tone had grown subdued and mollified, his voice, though still sounding disembodied, was now rising in tenor and tremor and the frequency of his nervous tic was increasing. What enabled me to detach myself from his provocative words and foil his intention to incite a third violent reaction was the fact that I no longer believed a word of what he was telling me. It now seemed to me to be obvious that Liam was delusional. I had concluded that he inhabited an extravagant fantasy world of his own creation.

'I did what Lisa had begged I do: I kept my distance,' he continued. 'I honoured my promise to her never to inform you of the truth about Andrew's parentage, thereby gifting you the biography that, by rights, was mine. How could I possibly bear the burden of such a sacrifice? You, of all people, should know. I buried my nose in book after book. For a while, reading helped to distract me from brooding over the sacrifice I'd made and imagining the endless fulfilment you must have felt with Lisa and Andrew sharing your life. But only for a while.

'After some years had dragged by, I arrived at the conclusion that a life lived incommunicado wasn't worth living and I decided to re-establish links with Lisa. By this time I'd grown frustrated by her treatment of me and was desperate to hear about Andrew. I'd found myself unable to think of much else beyond fantasising about Andrew and the conversations we'd have. It was only when I'd put pen to paper to write to Lisa that I thought of a way to get her to reply to my correspondence. I blackmailed her. Sometimes extremes are necessary. I wrote that unless she sent me a letter once a week containing news of Andrew, then I'd inform you that I was Andrew's father. So began our correspondence.

'For a while, Lisa's letters assuaged my feelings of loss — but I gradually realised that a regular supply of letters and the occasional photograph weren't enough. I needed to meet Andrew face to face. In the flesh. Initially, Lisa was horrified by this notion and had spouted forth all manner of objections in an attempt to dissuade me, but I was insistent till eventually, once I'd convinced her with countless reassurances concerning my capability for discretion and had repeated my threat to inform you of the truth about Andrew's parentage, she relented and effectively arranged a meeting by sending me details of the dates and the location of your accommodation in Majorca.

'You might recall that, on the first afternoon, while you were sunbathing on the beach, Lisa had opted to take Andrew shopping to buy him a bucket and spade. This was of course no more than a ruse to arrange a "chance" meeting at a café by the harbour where, for Andrew's sake, Lisa introduced me as a friend from America. I don't think Andrew believed this fiction for a moment, but he chose to play along with it. The fact that he didn't mention me to you, I think, supports my theory that he knew who I was right away. It was only when I encountered my own flesh and blood standing before me — a vital, vulnerable seven-year-old — that I realised the extent of the sacrifice I'd made. For Lisa, our meeting unexpectedly rekindled the mutual love that we'd both sought to deny throughout the intervening years. Her faith was visibly withering and, for a moment, I thought that I might be able to steal them both away from you. Indeed, that was the rash proposition I put to her and, though she didn't reject it outright, she did decline it the following day, though not without first declaring her love for me. I never did get the chance to reveal to Andrew my true identity — Lisa made it clear that were I to succumb to the temptation to do so, it would be the last time I would set eyes on him and she'd convinced me that, for the time being, it would not be in Andrew's best interests for me to reveal myself — but, as we were bidding our last farewells, we shared a moment of recognition and I knew he knew who I was and, therefore, who *he* was. That night I decided to abide by Lisa's ground rules and not identify myself to Andrew until he'd reached an age where I felt he could cope with such a revelation. I could have nourished myself with this thought for another decade. Already I was fantasising about informing Andrew on his seventeenth birthday that he was my son and indulged myself with visions of him deciding to abandon you and Lisa to come and live with me in New York. But, of course, that was not to be because, soon after, Andrew and Lisa were dead.'

I had sat and listened throughout the unravelling of this twisted fantasy, biding my time, garnering my strength, keeping my own counsel and seeking to conceal my mounting rage, but his perverse re-writing of reality was such that I lost the plot. I lunged at him for a third time and, finally wise to his manoeuvres, managed to make contact. My momentum overpowered his unprepared resistance and I grappled him to the ground and pummelled him. For a few moments I felt that I was gaining the upper hand. My surprise attack had exposed Liam's vulnerability and his struggle for breath betrayed the underlying fragility of his physical condition. But no sooner had his susceptibility become apparent than he seemed to tap into a hidden reserve of strength and the full force of his hostility was unleashed in a maelstrom that spewed forth from his lips and fists. He grabbed at the copies of *Original Harm* that had fallen from the shelves and used them to batter me over the head as he launched into a fresh tirade with renewed vigour.

'I knew straight away what had happened,' he roared. 'Lisa had informed you that she was leaving you for me and that she was taking Andrew with her. You'd had no premonition of Lisa's declaration of independence from you and your reaction to it was characteristically violent. You regarded her intention to seize control of her own biography as a humiliation as it trespassed upon your own status as the sole author of *yours*. You found the less-than-flattering characterisation of yourself contained within Lisa's biography as infringing to an unacceptable degree upon what you regarded as your fundamental right to pen your own portrait. Your temper flared briefly, but with fatal consequences. You grabbed the purple paperweight that had caught your eye in Soller market — I was there and I saw you buy it — and struck her with a single savage blow to the temple. When your rage had subsided and you saw the fatal consequences of your actions, under cover of darkness you disposed of Lisa's corpse by heaving it over the harbour wall and into the Mediterranean. But whilst you'd fabricated Lisa's death, and proceeded to re-write it in your head as suicide, Andrew's suicide was tragically all too genuine and entirely unforeseen. For all that you resented Andrew for displacing you in Lisa's affections, the overriding fact remained that he made you immortal, so that his death condemned you too to death everlasting. His death meant that the remainder of your own sorry excuse for a life would be forever misspent waiting for the arrival of your own inevitable full stop. For you to kill Andrew would have been tantamount to signing your own death warrant. No, whilst Lisa's death was undoubtedly murder, Andrew's was an unanticipated tragedy. You sought subsequently to come to terms with your overbearing burden of guilt in the only way you knew how — by writing about it — '

' — Lies!' I insisted.

' — Truth!' he yelled, hitting me over the head with a book. Then he stopped thumping me, cast the book aside and, wracked with grief, began to howl like a mortally wounded animal.

But it was me who was injured and there I lay, too weak to attempt an escape or a further attack, resigned to waiting for the culmination of this story, unsure whether it was mine or his anymore. As his anguish subsided to be substituted once again by anger, his nervous twitch punctuated the climaxing onslaught he delivered whilst tearing pages at random from the piles of books scattered around us.

'My reaction to Lisa and Andrew's deaths was the opposite of your own. You sought solace in words. I sought solace in action. You retreated from the real world. I attacked it head-on. I went to war to fight the good fight. For a decade. So what brought me back to you and why now?' he asked, reading me like a book again.

'This,' he answered himself, thrusting a copy of *Original Harm* into my face before resuming his wanton vandalism of any remaining copies within his reach.

'You cowardly hypocrite, entirely lacking any courage of conviction, who would publicly proclaim the sanctity of life in your bogus autobiography on the one hand whilst, on the other, furtively reducing the most precious gift that He gave us by putting words in the mouth of your thinly disguised alter ego, that anti-Christ mouthpiece Igor Harmnail (do me a favour!), to reduce it to nothing more than "a sexually transmitted terminal condition" that can and should be terminated on request! You, who would roundly mock my courageous, crusader Amino brothers and sisters, all of whom would die willingly for our beliefs; you, who believes in nothing, fabricates an autobiography that places yourself squarely on the moral high ground whilst murdering my own flesh and blood! You, who would savage *A Halo Ring Rim*, my extended love letter to you; who would slaughter my paean to an innocent, pure and tender spiritual love by warping and distorting it into a vile travesty through wholesale plagiarism: *Original* Harm? There's nothing original about it! Were you really so naive to think you could publish this infernal satire of *my* magnum opus and spare yourself damnation?'

At last I intuited Liam's intention and recognised him as my nemesis.

'I returned to make you eat your words,' he whispered in my ear, easing the first page into my mouth. I spat it out.

'Eat your words!' he screamed, stuffing pages down my throat. 'How could I stand by while you violated the memory of Lisa and Andrew in your plagiaristic parody of *my* words? This perverse attempt to absolve yourself of guilt by dedicating to your victims the very means by which you desecrate their legacy?'

The next thing that happened was so unexpected and so sudden that it still strikes me as surreal. Although it all happened in an instant, in my memory it occurs in slow motion. I remember Liam distracted by a piercing wail and turning to see Pardos, my would-be saviour, mid-flight, her teeth bared, pouncing on him. For an instant they were locked together in a momentous struggle, then Pardos sunk her teeth into his neck and drew blood. Enraged, Liam struck her. She crashed her head against a corner of the bookcase and crumpled to the floor alongside me. I scrambled over to her to determine the extent of her injuries and was stricken with horror when I found no sign of life.

In retrospect my forgetfulness remains inexplicable to me but it was only then, when I realised that I'd lost Pardos, that I remembered the skean dhu letter opener in my coat pocket. At once I unsheathed it and, before Liam had the chance to react, I had pounced on him and sliced his throat open from ear to ear, gutting him like an envelope.

The surprised expression on his face set a seal on my triumph over the destiny Liam had ghost-written for me. I had resumed my rightful place as author of my own story. Now that I'd regained control it was *my* turn to whisper into *his* ear.

'If Lisa *had* informed me that she was leaving me, as you say, might she not also have informed me — or maybe inadvertently let slip — that you were Andy's true father?' I whispered, for no other reason than to torture him with the cords of his own twisted logic. Then, as I listened to the strains of his dying breath, I bowed over him to ensure that I'd be heard and added, 'And, if so, then, correct me if I'm wrong, but surely that would mean that I'd have had no compunction about disposing of Andy too — wouldn't it? And that would mean that Andy's "suicide note" must have been written by someone else. Who could that have been I wonder?'

chapter twenty-three

a death sentence

I FOUND MYSELF MAROONED in the dead of calm that follows a storm leaving a landscape forever blighted by destruction in its wake. All was still. All was quiet. All the words that needed to be said had been said. There was nothing more to say and no one to say it to. I sat contemplating the bloody letter opener in my hand. I listened to myself breathe and tried to assimilate what had just happened. The more I thought about it, the more fictitious it seemed to me to be and I had to keep returning to the letter opener and the scene of death and destruction surrounding me to force myself to accept the indisputableness of the fact that what just happened *had happened*.

I fluctuated between a vertiginous sense of relief that all the anxiety that had been mounting since the receipt of Liam's first letter had been resolved and a spiralling tailspin of foreboding that, far from having reached a resolution, it had only just begun to accumulate. This eternity of morbid reflection and self-recrimination came to an abrupt conclusion when a possible escape clause occurred to me and I leapt to my feet and into action.

Moving with a swiftness and a precision borne of a determination unthinkable a moment earlier, I kissed Pardos's forehead, put my ear to her mouth and, neither hearing nor feeling any breath, transferred the letter opener from my hand into hers. I then emptied a sackful of rotting vegetables and filled it with all the copies of *Original Harm* I could find — taking care to retrieve every last one. Then I fled down the hillside and headed home to dispose of the sackful of books amongst the rest of the refuse at the bottom of the back green. It was only then that I permitted myself the luxury of a bath to soothe my aching limbs and attend to my numerous cuts and bruises. Then I poured myself a couple of stiff whiskies in an attempt to calm my jitters and rein in my racing mind.

Where did I go from here? I spent the remainder of the day and most of the night searching for, but never finding, a satisfactory answer. Instead, whilst my over-active mind replayed the events just described over and over again, I listened for a dreaded knock at the door and envisaged, all too vividly, the police breaking in, arresting me, dragging me down to the station, battering a confession out of me and throwing me in a cell where I slowly asphyxiated from a massive claustrophobia-induced asthma attack ignored by my brutal captors. This notion was, in itself, enough to trigger a real asthma attack, in the midst of which a means of finding an answer to the pressing question of which course of action I should now take occurred to me.

I picked up a pen and began to jot down what had happened to try and sort things out in my mind. The words I wrote are the words you've been reading. For all the drivel Liam had spouted about me — and, take my word for it, it *was* drivel — he was right about one thing: I *do* seek to write my way out of predicaments, even if, on occasion, I find subsequently that I've written my way into them.

The following morning I rolled out of bed, gulped down cornflakes, showered, shaved, shit and caught the 44 into work, scanning the paper en route. The front-page story told of how an intelligent missile had gone astray, exploding into a primary school, killing scores of children. I read the first couple of paragraphs then turned the page.

On disembarking, I headed straight for the office, my head still buried in the newspaper. It was only when I lifted it to behold the burnt-out shell of my former office block that I remembered the fire of the day before and made my way instead to the paper's temporary premises, where I took a deep breath and squeezed into a different but familiar crowded lift to the first floor. Once there, unable to resist the temptation, before I even removed my coat and hat, I stopped and glanced at the purple paperweight pinning down the pile of letters on my different but familiar desk.

As I rifled through the pile, one particular letter grabbed my attention. My name and address had been scrawled in familiar handwriting and I saw from the postmark that it had been posted locally the day before. I tore it open. As always, I'll reproduce the anonymous letter it contained for you verbatim:

I know you don't want to accept what I told you about Lisa and Andrew but, if you still doubt the truth, pay a visit to your doctor who will inform you of your impotence (a death sentence if ever there was one).

Reading this short letter, it struck me that perhaps my pet theory about how the consistency of the space left between words can be used to identify their author by acting as a kind of subconscious fingerprint might require some revision. This was because I could tell instantly that the wider-than-usual spaces between the words in this letter were the exact same as those in Andy's letter to you. My revised theory, therefore, is that the space we leave between the words we write is part of our genetic code, secreted within the amino acids handed down from one generation to the next.

'Morning,' sighed Kirsty Baird, teacup in hand, catching me off-guard on her way to the different but familiar kitchen.

'Morning,' I obliged.

'How's the missus?' she asked. I hesitated a moment before answering her.

'Fine,' I smiled. 'She's fine.'

chapter twenty-four

the footnote

MY INITIAL REACTION to receiving this death sentence was an instinctive sense of freedom, followed by a feeling of weightless worthlessness. I felt as if the arch-villain in the film of my auto-biography had bent the director's ear and swapped roles with me so that he was now cast as the tragically heroic male lead whilst I was consigned to play the walk-on part I'd sketched out for him. I felt as if I'd been reduced to a footnote, a one-dimensional character in my own autobiography. I did not live and breathe. I was not flesh and blood. I amounted to no more than words on a page in a book nobody read.

And then it occurred to me that, whilst I might be writing these very words for myself, in an attempt to make some kind of sense of it all, I'm also writing them for you — and that was the moment when a means of resurrection, an ingenious way to reclaim the lead role, struck me: by casting you as my female lead.

Oh, I know that this might come as something of a shock — and if I didn't know that we already knew each other intimately (if only through our correspondence) then some might consider it somewhat presumptuous — but the wonderful fact is that I've already fled my previous life, consigned it to history, to start afresh, here, with you!

On impulse, suddenly unable to bear the thought of Kirsty Baird's innocent enquiry about my missus for a single day more, I packed my bags and boarded the first available flight to Toronto on a one-way ticket to hitchhike my way across Canada to be with you in Vancouver Island.

And as I sit here in a solitary cabin somewhere in the Rockies, struggling to express my thoughts into these last words, before embarking on the last leg of my journey to you, my ultimate destination, I find myself distracted by the view of the snow-capped mountains rising out of the deep green and brown forest to pierce the bluest sky framed by the window and I inhale the all-encompassing emptiness. I'm surrounded by nothing. And nothing matters to me. Anymore. Except you.

There's nothing to do here but write. And read. I've found ample time to re-read *Original Harm* and *A Halo Ring Rim* and have discovered that, not only had Liam's diatribe been sprinkled with fragments lifted straight from *Original Harm* but that these self-same phrases also appear within *A Halo Ring Rim*. Was this coincidental, or had I subconsciously plagiarised him?

I know what Pardos's response to such speculation would be, but then Pardos is dead.

I've also found time to re-read a lot of old letters and, in retrospect, I can see now that I've known, from the first time I'd read your first letter, that it was our destiny to be together: letters I'd written to Liam; letters Liam had written to me; letters Andy had written to you; letters you'd written to Andy; letters I'd written to you under the guise of Andy and letters you'd written to Andy (me). It was the need to confess this deception — masquerading as my own dead son — that was part of the impetus behind penning these words. But I know that you'll forgive me, won't you?

Oh, I know that your bookshelves, like mine, are heaving with unreliable narrators but, trust me, I'm not one of them. Liam was right about many things — the need to live rather than spend a lifetime reading and writing about life — but, I implore you to believe me, he was mistaken about me.

Oh, the anticipation of being able, finally, to read the letters that Andy had written to you; to gain insight into both sides of the story! And, at last, I can deliver, in person, Andy's precious last letter to you.

And so here I find myself, in self-imposed solitary confinement, the bloody vigour of sheer excitement coursing through my veins as, impatiently, I count down the days and nights and hours till, at last, that momentous moment arrives when we meet, finally, in the flesh!

But now, at last, I've had my fill of words. I've arrived at the conclusion that the words left unwritten are as important as those that are. Of at least equal importance is the ability to read between the lines.

It's time for me to take a leaf out of Liam's book; to forsake words for flesh and blood. Oh Marina, perhaps together we can find a way to elude the death sentence of the full stop? Maybe the end of this story can mark the beginning of a new chapter in both our lives? Let us together, you and I, take a leap of faith and jump off the page…

chapter twenty-five

a new chapter

Acknowledgement

Thanks to Craig Hillsley for helping to extricate me from the tangled web within which I'd contrived to ensnare myself.